RESCUED BY MARRIAGE

BY
DIANNE DRAKE

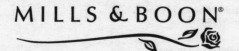

First published in Great Britain 2006
Harlequin Mills & Boon Limited,
Eton House, 18-24 Paradise Road, Richmond, Surrey TW9 1SR

© Dianne Despain 2006

ISBN-13: 978 0 263 84755 0
ISBN-10:   0 263 84755 1

Set in Times Roman 10½ on 12½ pt
03-0906-57386

Printed and bound in Spain
by Litografia Rosés, S.A., Barcelona

"So what you're saying here is that I distract you?"

He gave her an innocently sexy grin—one that would have melted her resolve if she'd let it. But she wouldn't, and she averted her eyes to be safe from the kind of distraction that shocked her...the physical kind, the kind that looked at Sam in a way other than someone to lean on.

"You distract me in more ways than you know," she whispered. "And I can't allow that to happen, because I have another priority."

"I suppose you're not going to tell me what that is?"

Della shook her head. "No. This is *my* life and I've got to learn to get along in it. You'll be gone in another couple of weeks anyway. I'm sorry, Sam."

"So am I, Della. For more reasons than you know, so am I."

Now that her children have left home, **Dianne Drake** is finally finding the time to do some of the things she adores—gardening, cooking, reading, shopping for antiques. Her absolute passion in life, however, is adopting abandoned and abused animals. Right now Dianne and her husband Joel have a little menagerie of three dogs and two cats, but that's always subject to change. A former symphony orchestra member, Dianne now attends the symphony as a spectator several times a months and, when time permits, takes in an occasional football, basketball or hockey game. Dianne loves to hear from readers, so feel free to e-mail her at DianneDrake@earthlink.net

Recent titles by the same author:

EMERGENCY IN ALASKA
THE DOCTOR'S COURAGEOUS BRIDE *24:7*
THE SURGEON'S RESCUE MISSION *24:7*

RESCUED BY MARRIAGE

CHAPTER ONE

FOSTER ARMSTRONG slid the offer across the table to Della Riordan with an anxious smile. "It's the best offer you're going to get. In my opinion, for the money, it's quite a bargain."

He was correct, it probably was. One medical practice, one medical office and one house on rolling acreage. Actually, it was much more than she thought she'd be able to manage, which was why she was still a bit hesitant about this deal. It seemed too good to be true, and she simply didn't have the money to gamble if that's how it turned out. This was their future after all—hers and Meghan's. There was no room in it to make a drastic mistake.

Except for her own little pittance of a nest egg she'd had tucked away when Anthony had died three months ago, Della had very little else to get herself going again. Anthony had seen to that quite handily, which had come as quite a shock. Barely one day after being widowed, Della had learned that her husband had left them virtually penniless with, quite literally, only the clothes on their backs and a handful of personal items. On top of that, he'd acquired more debt than Della had known about, debt she could still barely even comprehend, debt she was going to be forced to make good on. It wasn't like she was dumb about these things—she'd always balanced the household books and even assisted with the clinic financial records. But Anthony had been deceitful about his spending. He'd been a successful surgeon and an amazing doctor overall. But he'd also been a liar and a cheat, and ev-everything he'd been to Della had merely been an illusion. Smoke and mirrors.

For all their eight years of marriage, Anthony Riordan had been living well beyond his means and hiding every speck of it from his wife. That, and a high-style mistress or two along the way.

"It's a bargain," she said tentatively. "And I'm definitely tempted by it." And the good thing about Redcliffe Island was that it was a thousand miles away from Anthony's family. But that was the bad thing, too, because they had Meghan in their custody now, and a thousand miles would be such a stagger-ing distance from her daughter. Even thinking about it brought a sharp pang to Della's heart. The loneliness seeped in so easily these days without Meghan, and she spent most of her time in the very depths of despair over what she'd lost because of Anthony—not the house, not the cars, not the furniture, not the boat. She'd lost Meghan, and for that she would never forgive him. "So let me get this straight. If I agree to the terms, the residents of the island will chip in and subsidize half of the cost? Just like that, they're going to pay half the fee to buy the medical practice from their former doctor simply to get me there?"

The balding, middle-aged, serious-looking man opposite her smiled. "That's the offer they've made. They haven't had a resident doctor in years, and they want one, so it looks like they'll do whatever's necessary to get one there, including sub-sidizing half the cost of the medical practice, if that's what it takes to make the offer look appealing. What else can I say? They have a need and so do you. Perfect match, the way I see it."

"And it's only two miles off the mainland? This Redcliffe Island is only two miles away?" The idea of a small island was a little claustrophobic, she thought, but if she could get away to the mainland every now and then, it wouldn't be so bad.

"Two miles, and many of the people do commute back and forth every day. There's a regular commuter ferry so it's not like you're going to be completely cut off from the world." He chuckled. "Electricity, running water, indoor plumbing, all the comforts of civilization come included. There's nothing at all backward about the place."

At this point in her life, if it was a fresh start that would get Meghan back, backward wouldn't matter. Della looked at the contract again. This could be the perfect solution. Set up a practice, prove she was a fit mother. "And they do realize I'm only a general practitioner?" She hadn't gone far enough in her education to have a specialty. After graduating medical school, she'd gone straight to an internship and from there straight into labor and delivery…as the patient, not the doctor. Consequently, she'd had no specialty training, which meant the hospitals didn't want her. Neither did any clinics because a general practitioner with only public health experience wasn't exactly in high demand. "No specialty whatsoever."

"They know your credentials, and you do come highly recommended by your clinic. If the islanders need a specialist, they'll go to the mainland for one. They're fine with that arrangement."

Della sighed. She was very tempted… Still, when it sounded too good to be true, it usually was. Right now, this *still* sounded much too good to be true. She'd already learned the lesson—Anthony Riordan had been too good to be true the first time she'd laid eyes on him. Now look what she had to show for that! She was practically penniless, nearly homeless, jobless, and her daughter in the custody of Anthony's parents until she straightened out her life. "Can I have some time to think about it?"

Foster Armstrong smiled patiently. "I've been authorized to leave this deal on the table for one day only. Twenty-four hours. After that you're still welcome to buy the medical practice and all that goes with it, but the subsidies donated by the island will not be part of the deal, I'm sorry to say."

Della blinked her surprise. "They're putting me on a timeline?"

He shrugged. "I'm only the agent. That was part of their proposition and I'm not empowered to change the provisions. I expect it's eagerness, most likely."

She hoped so, because that rush was an added worry. Of course, affordability was an even bigger worry because without the subsidy she wouldn't be able to afford the practice, which would put the total package out of her reach. Prior to this she'd looked at a couple other options—small town and rural practices—and couldn't come close to touching those. The next option would have been to start her own practice from the ground up, but she simply didn't have the money, not to mention the fact that if she did that there would be no guarantee of patients coming to her. It might take months or years to get a good start. So buying an established practice was the way to go, if she could find one she was able to afford. Which seemed to be the medical practice on Redcliffe Island.

"That's not a lot of time, especially since if I accept this I'll be changing my whole life."

It wasn't enough time to make arrangements to go take a look at what she might be buying, either. But she'd worked in a public health clinic in Miami, one with practically no facilities, no supplies, and many more patients than were manageable. So how horrible could something on rolling acreage, according to the papers, be compared to that?

"No, it's not a lot of time, Doctor, but it is a lot of generosity. And there are no strings attached except that you stay for five years. That's all they're asking. Five years in exchange for full title of your practice and properties."

"You don't happen to have any pictures, do you? Of the house I'll be getting? Or even the medical office?" The contract stipulated office and all equipment, but it didn't state what that equipment would be.

He shook his head. "Sorry. I don't. This listing has only just been handed over to me, and so far I've managed this only from my office and haven't actually been to the property."

She nodded. Pictures would have been nice, but the view from the kitchen window she was buying wasn't the essential thing here. What was essential was the ability to walk in and assume the role of physician to an established patient base. Which was exactly what this offer was. Built-in patients, ready and eager for a doctor. "And this practice has been on the market for how long?"

"A rather long time. Two years, I believe." To make sure, Foster Armstrong put on his half-glasses and searched through the packet of papers he had with him. "Actually, it's closer to three years," he said, then cleared his throat. "It's been listed that long but, according to what I see here, there haven't been any serious offers. A few looks, a couple of weak considerations, a reneged offer, but nothing gainful. Fred Barnes, the man who handled this matter before I took it over, left a note to the effect that because the practice is relatively small, which will limit the income potential, he believed that was the predominant factor in the lack of interest." He looked up from the document, staring intently at Della over the tops of his glasses. "But you told me that you don't require a tremendous financial gain from this venture, only enough to support you and your daughter, and this practice will most certainly do that.

Then when you consider that it comes with the house for the two of you, I think it's a good match for your needs. Especially since you don't have the means to afford much else."

Her needs. She had only one. Get Meghan back. The judge had said she had to prove stability in her life if she wanted custody again. Three months ago, she'd had all the stability in the world—a husband, a mansion in Miami, a wonderful job in a public health clinic and Meghan. How much more stable could anyone be? "You said I'm obligated to five years. What happens if I don't stick it out?"

"You pay the islanders back their share of the investment at the time you sell the practice. No penalties involved."

"But what happens if they don't like me and won't come to me for their medical services?"

"They pay you back for your expenditure, which is an extraordinary clause, and they'll sell the practice themselves. In all the years I've been brokering these deals, I've never had one like it. But the island advisory board likes your résumé and I seriously doubt you're going to have a problem with them *not* wanting to use your services. In fact, they're willing to fly you to Massachusetts and take you over to the island as soon as you can get there. Tomorrow, even."

She wasn't prepared for that. Wasn't prepared to say goodbye to Meghan yet. But the sooner she got started, the sooner she would have her daughter back. She hoped. The judge had set six months for a review of Meghan's custody, and three weeks of that had already ticked off the clock as she explored her options. "I'll need my car."

"They'll provide one until yours can be sent over."

"And my furniture." What there was of it. She'd bought a few pieces for that one-room apartment she and Meghan had been living in since Anthony's death. A bed, a couch, a table.

"They'll have it shipped."

"I won't have a lot of money for start-up expenses in the office."

"They'll make you a generous loan, or take care of other arrangements as needed to get you started. And much of the equipment you'll need is in storage, according to the papers."

"Other arrangements?"

He nodded. "They're committed to doing whatever it takes to give you your start. I'm under the impression that their needs are basic and they don't care about extravagance and image, so as long as you're a good doctor for them you're not going to have to worry about a fancy, up-to-date office and the newest medical gadgets on the market. In other words, they'll help you get the basics you'll need."

"That's good, because I'll be lucky to manage the basics." This was getting more and more tempting, and maybe the only reason she was hesitating was that she simply didn't trust anyone any more. She'd trusted her husband once and he'd betrayed her in more ways than she would have ever guessed he could. Then his parents had betrayed her on top of that. They'd always been gracious and supportive, especially after the funeral, when she'd found out Anthony had left her practically destitute. Of course, while they had been supportive they had also been filing for Meghan's custody behind her back, using the small amount of money she'd accepted from them to help herself get going again as the proof that she was unable to take proper care of her daughter. Begging for handouts was what the Riordans had officially called it in the court papers. Begging... She hadn't even wanted the money but she'd accepted it to spare Meghan the rift. *Accepted*, not asked or begged for!

Her mind wandered to that awful day in court, as it had so many times since then. "She works in a free clinic and doesn't receive a regular salary," Vivian Riordan had told the judge.

Which was true. She did. But when Anthony had been alive, finances hadn't been an issue and it hadn't mattered. At least, she hadn't thought it did at the time. "And she's gotten rid of her babysitter so now she takes my granddaughter to work with her in that clinic. It's no fit place for a child to spend her day, playing among all those sick people." True in part. She couldn't afford the babysitter now. She could barely afford their one-room apartment. And, yes, Meghan had gone to work with her, but Della always kept her separated from the patients. It had been the best she could manage under the circumstances and, selfishly, she had enjoyed having more time with her daughter.

Not only had Anthony, and Anthony's parents, betrayed her, the judge had, too, when he'd taken away her little girl. Somehow she'd never equated her meager lifestyle to being a bad parent, but he had. He'd looked at what had been taken away from Meghan and not what Meghan still had—a mother who cherished her and would do whatever it took to provide for her. Then he'd pronounced Della an unworthy parent and had given her six months in which to make herself worthy again.

So now, after all those betrayals, Della simply didn't trust. She couldn't. Which was holding her back from accepting this offer. She'd accepted the Riordans' generosity and it had cost her Meghan. With this offer now, all she could wonder about was the real cost.

"Twenty-four hours, Dr Riordan. Then the offer is off the table."

"I understand." So many things could happen in twenty-four hours. A husband could die. His adulterous affairs could be exposed. The solicitors could give you seventy-two hours in which to vacate your home because it, and everything in it, were going into foreclosure to pay for your husband's extravagant habits.

Or, in twenty-four hours, the road to a new life could unfold. "I'll let you know first thing tomorrow morning," she said.

"I'll be anxious to hear your decision, Dr Riordan."

"So will I, Mr Armstrong. So will I."

Twenty-four hours later

She'd cried all the way from Miami to Boston. Sniffled off and on, and a couple times broken into out and out sobs. It had got so bad the man sitting in the seat next to her on the airplane had asked the flight attendant for another seat. Then she'd cried at the baggage claim, at the taxi stand and all the way up the coast to Connaught, the tiny little harbor town where she'd caught the boat over to Redcliffe.

Naturally, she'd cried all the way over to Redcliffe, too, and now, as they approached the island, and her face was bloated and red, she was afraid the people there would take one look at her and send her back. But, damn it, she already missed Meghan. She'd missed her even before her last goodbye kiss. And it wasn't like the Riordans wouldn't take good care of her. They adored her and they would take very good care. But Meghan wasn't theirs to care for, and leaving her behind with them was the hardest thing Della had ever done in her life. It hurt far worse than losing her husband had, but by that point in the marital relationship she had been practically void of feelings for him anyway. She would have been totally void of feelings had she known then about all his proclivities and what they would cost her.

She looked out to the dock. About a dozen people were mingling there. "They wouldn't happen to be waiting there for someone else to arrive, would they?" she asked Cecil, the captain of this boat. He was an older gent, weather-beaten face, bushy beard, genuine smile.

"They've been anxious ever since they heard you'd agreed to the offer. It's not always convenient to go across the water to the doctor, especially when the weather turns bad. Makes a body sicker than it was just to get there and back. So they were mighty glad when you accepted."

Twenty-two hours ago had been when she'd accepted. She hadn't taken much time to think it over because it was this or, well, she didn't know what. Something else would have turned up eventually, but there was no predicting how long *eventually* would have taken. And six months minus three weeks wasn't an awfully long time in which to start over and make a go of it. So she'd accepted, spent the evening at Meghan's kindergarten play then packed up and stepped onto the airplane. "What happened to the last doctor?"

"Went to the big city. New York, I think. I didn't talk to him myself, but I heard he didn't like being isolated all the way out there by himself. Not married, no one around…"

"He didn't live in the village?"

"No, ma'am."

He said that like she should have already known it, and suddenly she wondered what else Foster Armstrong had failed to mention. Or perhaps hadn't known to mention.

"Is it awfully far from the village?" Suddenly, she was seeing the village at one end of the island and her house all the way at the other, with nothing but wilderness in between. That was a very sobering thought for a city girl. Sobering and daunting.

Cecil chuckled, and his beard bobbed up and down. "No, ma'am. Nothing on the island is far from the village as long as there's a good road to take you there."

"Would there happen to be a good road to take me where I'm going?"

"Nice little road, actually. Used to be well traveled when

Doc Bonn lived out there. Even when Docs Beaumont and Weatherby were there. I expect it grew up some over the years."

"Three years since the last doctor," she stated.

"More like three and a half, if I recall."

Curiosity was getting the better of her now. "How long was he here before he left?"

"Don't rightly remember for sure, but I think five, maybe six…"

"Years?"

He shook his head. "Weeks. Not quite as long as Doc Weatherby. He lasted three…"

"Years?"

"No, ma'am. Months. Three months, give or take a few days."

"And it took Dr Beaumont all this time to sell his practice?"

"Funny how that turned out, because it took Doc Weatherby almost that long, too. Both times the island finally resorted to pitching in."

Della looked down at the boat deck to see if her heart had just sunk through the boards, because it sure felt like it did. Then she started to cry again as they chugged slowly into the harbor.

She wasn't what he'd expected. Not at all. Somehow, he'd pictured the next doctor on Redcliffe to be a large woman. Stout. Rough and tough. But she was tiny. Barely five feet, blond hair. Delicate. Sam Montgomery stepped back into the crowd awaiting her arrival and watched Dr Della Riordan step off Captain Cecil's boat and take a good, long look at her surroundings. She wasn't at all sure of herself, either. And…was that a horrible allergy going on with her? Her face was red and puffy, her eyes swollen, and she was blotting her nose like she belonged in bed, under the covers, vaporizer going, sipping hot chicken and noodle soup. She had to be sick, and other than the fact that she looked like someone who needed an IV and oxygen, she was probably very pretty.

Poor thing. She was about to be mobbed and the doctor in him wanted to do something to help her out of that spot. But the doctor in him was also charged to stand back and simply observe. Then report. He wasn't to be obtrusive, wasn't to be particularly helpful. Some involvement was acceptable but not so much that he actually had a say, or a way in how the new doctor would set up her practice. All that because the previous medical practices here had such a spotty history, the medical board was keen to see this one done to proper standards. In other words, it was a test that came about because of prior bad experiences—a protection for the residents who could be too eager to accept a doctor who might not serve their best interests. They did have that history here, taking in a doctor who didn't suit them.

So, according to the area health commissioner, the only thing Sam was supposed to do was make sure the new doctor set up her clinic to standard. Or provide enough evidence to shut her down if she didn't. Simple task, and that's what he did now. No more patient care. All observation and reports. Which made his life quite simple.

But, damn it, the islanders were hoisting this poor doctor up onto a platform and asking her to say a few words, when she looked like she wanted to do anything but that. It was amazing they hadn't hauled out a brass band for the occasion. And she looked so…he wasn't sure what. It wasn't fear, wasn't even fatigue. Sadness, maybe? "So I suppose I should rescue the doctor in distress," he muttered, stepping through the nearly fifty people who had now gathered for the welcome.

"I'm glad to be here," she said to the village mayor as he

pumped her hand the way only a six-foot-seven mountain of a man could do.

"And we're glad to have you here, Doc Riordan," Mayor Bruce Vargas responded.

"Call me Della."

"Doc Della," he said. "The village of Redcliffe is anxious to have you set up and going, and we're ready to do anything required to help you."

"Dr Riordan and I have some medical matters to discuss," Sam Montgomery said, stepping up to the platform. "I hate to break this up and I know everybody's thrilled to have her here, but before she can start her practice we have some issues to go over about health-care requirements in Massachusetts." Whatever that meant, since he really was quite far removed from the real medical world now. He looked directly at Della. "I'm Dr Sam Montgomery," he said, extending his hand to her.

She nodded, and took his hand, but didn't say a word.

"You look like you could use a cup of coffee." Or a shot of penicillin and a week in bed.

She nodded. "That would be nice." But she didn't smile, and the only word he could think of to describe what he was seeing was heartbreak. Dr Della Riordan was suffering from a broken heart. No wonder she'd been so quick to accept this offer. Why else would anybody want to come to Redcliffe to practice medicine if they weren't trying to get away from something?

The tiny bit of the village she saw looked nice enough. The main street was quaint, with its tidy Cape Cod style predominant in the architecture. The people here smiled at each other and exchanged pleasant greetings. The air was pure and crisp. And the ride over on Captain Cecil's boat hadn't been bad at all in the salty breeze—what she'd seen of it through the tears. All good signs, but none of them did anything to alleviate her pain. She already missed Meghan so badly she wasn't sure she could survive the next five minutes away from her, let alone the next five months. But if she turned around now and went right back to Miami with even less than she'd had when she'd left there… No, that wasn't an alternative. She had to make this situation work, no matter what it was she'd gotten herself into.

"I appreciate the coffee," she said, sliding into the booth across from Sam as he waved for the waitress. "I've had a long twenty-four hours and I think it's finally catching up with me. This time yesterday I'd barely even heard of Redcliffe Island except for what I'd read in the offer papers, and now I'm a resident here for the next five years. It's a lot to deal with in the span of a day."

"One of those strange twists of fate. This time yesterday I'd barely even heard of Redcliffe Island, either. And now everybody here knows my name."

"They are friendly, aren't they?" she said, her voice on the edge of a tremble. He seemed nice. Handsome, for sure. Wavy brown hair, dark brown eyes. Fetching build, too. Probably around six feet tall, he cut a handsome figure in his casual jeans and T-shirt, and she especially liked his relaxed smile. She thought about Anthony for a moment. Nothing about him had ever been casual or relaxed. He'd been the epitome of starched and polished perfection and he'd had quite the sharp edge to his beau ideal. She couldn't recall ever having seen him in a T-shirt and jeans in all their years of marriage, let alone sitting in a cozy, comfortable diner, sipping coffee. No, he had been too upscale for such a thing.

"Would you like something to eat?" Sam offered. "A sandwich, maybe a cup of chowder?"

She shook her head. Truth was, it was easier not to eat. The way she'd felt so much of the time lately, there wasn't much point since whatever she ate merely turned into a nauseated muddle in the pit her stomach. "So, what, exactly, do you do here? I was led to believe I was the only doctor on the island."

"Technically, you are. But I'm here from the state health commission, basically to make sure your transition into your new practice is a smooth one. Redcliffe has a peculiar history with its doctors, so I'll be around for a while to…to assist you where I can, I suppose you could say."

"What, exactly, is this peculiar history, other than their doctors not staying?"

"You don't know?"

She shook her head, although she wasn't about to tell him she'd bought the practice on a whim. A very fast, possibly very foolish whim.

"Like you already know, nobody wants to stay. The people are nice, the island is a veritable Atlantic paradise, but I think the past few doctors have found the island to be a little more off the beaten path than they expected. Quite restrictive, I think. When you hear paradise you think of glamorous, and nothing here is about glamor. Also, the earning potential is not nearly as great as it might be on the mainland, just a few miles away. Personally, I think that's a huge factor in the reason no one wants to stay. Then there's the isolation…some people aren't cut out for it. And it's quite isolated, as you already know. Which is what surprises me about you coming here…alone. You are alone, aren't you?"

"For now," she said, sighing. "And I came here because I want to be off the beaten path." That much was absolutely true. She wanted to set up her new life without the Riordans' interference, and interference was a distinct likelihood if she did it under their scrutiny.

"Then you've come to the right place because I'm not even sure if there is a beaten path."

"Speaking of the right place, I'd like to go find it and get myself settled in. Do you know where it is?"

He raised his eyebrows skeptically. "You don't?"

"I'm not very good at directions." That was a bit of a hedge, but there was no reason to include him in every little detail of her business transaction. Truth was, buying what she had, sight unseen, might seem a little strange to most people, and what she didn't want was for word to get around that the new doctor was wonky in such affairs, because that could get back to the judge. So instead of admitting that quite possibly she was wonky, or worse, she merely smiled. "I get myself lost at the end of my driveway and right now I'm not even sure if I go left or right to get there."

"Then we'll go pick up your loaner car from the mayor, and you can follow me on out there."

She wanted to ask how far *on out* was, but instead she took another sip of coffee. It didn't matter anyway. However far it was, she owned it, and for the next five years it was going to be her home sweet home. In a little over five months, home sweet home for Meghan, too. That, and nothing else, was what mattered.

CHAPTER TWO

THE loaner car was nice—a compact little SUV. Purple. The mayor explained that it belonged to his daughter who was off to college right now, and Della's first thought was why would a college girl need a car on Redcliffe Island? Was there anyplace to go here? Of course, she didn't ask. That would have been impolite. Instead, she accepted the keys graciously and promised to be careful.

"I might stop in to see you later," Mayor Vargas said, as he rubbed his shoulder. "Got a little touch of arthritis setting in, I'm afraid. Maybe you could take a look."

Her first patient. This was promising. Here less than an hour and she was about to get busy. "Stop by any time." She assumed he knew where to stop by, and she would have told him to call for an appointment, but she didn't know if her phone service was in operation yet. Land-line phone. She'd given up her cellphone right after she'd given up just about everything else that had added an extra bill to her burden. In her old life the cost of it hadn't mattered; in her new life it did tremendously. "I'll be glad to have a look at you." She was tempted to tell him to bring all his friends along for an exam, too, but that would have seemed rather bold of her.

"So, is there anything else we can do to help you get settled in, Doc?" he asked. "I know some of the ladies are going to bring meals to you for a while, until you're set up on your own."

"I hadn't even thought about that," she admitted. "I appreciate it."

"Well, that's the way we operate here. What's mine is yours…you know how that is."

She smiled like she did know. But the truth was, all those years she'd been married to Anthony she'd thought what had been his had been hers, too, and that everything in their marriage had been shared. Which hadn't turned out to be the case. It had all been his, except the debt, and that had become all hers.

"So are we good to go?" Sam asked.

"Do I need a key or something to get into the house or the clinic?" Della asked, suddenly realizing that she had nothing that marked ownership or entitlement to the house or property other than the word of Foster Armstrong, who'd said he would send the papers along once they were registered.

"It's open," the mayor said, then bade them goodbye and scurried off to his office.

Della stood on the sidewalk for a moment, simply looking around. She liked it, she thought. It was easy. People were friendly. Strangers waved and smiled, and old men tipped their hats in polite greeting. Maybe being cut off from the mainstream wasn't such a bad thing. "So you've never been here before?" she asked Sam.

Sam shook his head. "I'm new in the job. Got lots of territory to cover, and I haven't had time before now. Without a doctor on the island, I didn't have a reason, either."

"You don't practice medicine at all?"

"Not for an awfully long time. It ties you to one place, and I don't like to be tied any more." He flashed an extraordinarily sexy grin at her. "Been there, done that, moved on to something else. Life's too short to be stuck with something you don't want."

"I like having roots. It's nice to have the same place to come home to. There's something comforting in stability." She realized that more now than she ever had before.

"We all think that at some time, I suppose. I did once, but I was wrong about it… For me it was wrong, anyway. So, why don't you and that purple car follow me out to your house and we'll see if we can get you set up to stay before it gets too late." He glanced around. "Where are your things?"

She pointed to her duffle bag, a suitcase and the hand grip next to it. "That's it. Pretty much everything I own. I'm having a few things sent up from Miami shortly, but I traveled light."

He gave her an odd look, one somewhere between concern and shock. "Are you sure you know what you're getting yourself into? Because right now I think maybe we should find you a place at one of the local bed and breakfasts until the rest of your things arrive."

A bed and breakfast for the night sounded wonderful—a nice cozy room with a comfy mattress, fresh muffins and juice in the morning. The whole esthetic New England appeal suddenly embraced her, but, as much as she would have loved to be pampered in it, she couldn't afford it. Which was none of Sam's business. Besides, the sooner she got to her new home, the sooner she would start work on her new life. "I'll be fine," she said. "I don't require much to get by."

"Apparently you don't." He gave her an indifferent shrug, then headed across the street to his SUV—a black one that was about three times the size of hers. "Suit yourself," he called back, as he hopped inside.

Suit herself… If that had been an option, suiting herself would have included being with Meghan. Being *anywhere* with Meghan. Thinking about her brought the tears up again and before they started to roll, Della climbed into her purple runabout and fell in behind Sam Montgomery. Why would a man like him avoid the roots when all she wanted in this life was to have them back?

He was trying to get away from something, she decided. Bad experience in the past had him on the run. "Aren't we all?" she said aloud as the tiny village of Redcliffe, which was the hub of life on Redcliffe Island, turned into a speck in her rear-view mirror.

About a mile down the road, Della followed Sam onto another road, then another and another until she started to wonder if they were caught up in some sort of a maze. They had to be going in circles, and what was more astonishing was that there was simply no sign of life out here. Once Redcliffe was behind her, except for the occasional dot of a cottage along the roadway, civilization seemed to stop. If not for the actual roads, this could have been considered uncharted territory. "So, it seems I'm going to be a country girl." That was a bit of a concern, since she'd hardly ever been into the rural reaches—not even for a Sunday drive.

But this could be a good thing, couldn't it? An isolated little place without distractions might be perfect, exactly what the doctor ordered. Besides, the scenery along the way was beautiful. Stunning. On the left a lush, green pasture cascaded over a craggy area and Della saw cows grazing peacefully. Then up ahead there was an orchard of some kind. Apples, perhaps? If they were, maybe she and Meghan could spend a day picking apples and baking pies and tarts, and making apple sauce from them. She was the right age to start helping in the kitchen, Della thought. In Miami they'd either eaten out or brought cooked meals in. No one had used the kitchen except to make coffee or tea or fix an occasional bowl of cereal. Suddenly, Della was excited about what she and Meghan might do together in a nice little kitchen.

No, this wasn't the city, which was all she knew, but it was nice. Beautiful. Peaceful. In a way, it seemed almost un-touched. She and Meghan could be happy here…at least for five years. That thought put a smile on her face as she followed Sam into yet another turn. After a short distance they passed through something that looked like junk or maybe metal statuary lining the road. She twisted to look, and almost collided with Sam's SUV, which came to a stop on a knoll just past all the litter. Or was it art?

Turning her attention back to what was beyond her wind-shield, Della saw a house, but it wasn't hers. It couldn't be. This one was a dilapidated old Victorian one-story, with peeling white paint and gingerbread decoration dangling off the eaves in some places and completely missing in others. It was weathered and old. A lovely lady in her day, but her day was long gone. The beach beyond her was stunning, though, with its white sand and billowing grasses.

"Why are we stopping?" she called to Sam, who was already out of his car, leaning causally against it. Something in the pit of her stomach already told her she knew the answer, but she needed to hear it said. *It's another of your mistakes, Della. The biggest one of all.*

"We're stopping because this is the end of the road," he called back.

Another bitter reality hit home. Sticking her head out the window, Della inhaled, filling her lungs with the fresh salt air. It was different from the salt air in Miami—cleaner, maybe. No smell of civilization mixed in with it, and it was a pleasant surprise because it reminded her of trips to the beach with Meghan.

"You've changed your mind and decided to stay in a bed and breakfast?" he asked, when she didn't get out of the SUV immediately.

"No. I'm staying in my house." Such as it was. Now she

understood why Drs Beaumont and Weatherby had pulled out of here so quickly. And the house had had so many more years since then to become even more rundown. If she hadn't already cried all her tears over missing Meghan, she would have cried a few right here over this mess.

"You've never been here, have you?" Sam asked stepping up to her car and leaning through the window.

What was she supposed to tell him? That she was the biggest idiot in the world, the one who would spend the next five years in this hovel? And how was she supposed to practice medicine here? "I'm not put off by hard work," she said, hoping that sounded sufficiently in control.

"I thought it was a little odd that someone had actually bought this place with the intent of setting up practice here again. But, then, some people are handy. They like to take on projects. Although, since I didn't see a carpenter's belt among your possessions, I'm guessing you don't."

"Maybe I simply like my solitude."

"Then it's a good thing, because you're going to get plenty of it out here. So, which do you want to see first? Your house or your clinic?"

"You don't have to show me anything," she said, trying to sound confident, even though she knew she sounded more defeated than anything. This was all she had now and there was no way she could turn it into something that would win her custody of her daughter. From the plain pumpkin into the beautiful Cinderella coach…she didn't have the magical wand she needed for the transformation. Sighing, Della shut her eyes to hold in the tears. "I'm fine," she said. "Thank you for leading me out here. You don't have to stay."

"The bed and breakfast where I've booked a room has one empty down the hall from me. I'm sure Mrs Hawkins would be glad to have you move in there until…until you can spruce this place up, if that's what you decide to do with it."

"Spruce it up?" Della laughed bitterly. Now she had to spruce up her house like she was trying to spruce up her life. Damn Anthony Riordan for getting her into this.

Sam couldn't believe it! She hadn't known. She truly hadn't known the condition of this place. So what would possess someone to buy this medical practice and everything that went with it sight unseen? Frankly, she didn't seem like the type. In fact, she seemed quite the opposite—down to earth, steady, sensible. Of course, looks were deceiving, weren't they? He glanced down at his empty ring finger, empty a year now. There wasn't even the faint trace of a wedding ring left any more. "Look, Della, we've got to do something here. Without prying into why you did it, I do know you bought this practice without ever having been here, and I'm guessing that it was never your intention to take this on as a fixer-upper. Is that much true?"

She nodded, but didn't speak.

"Maybe whoever you bought it from will refund your money?" Which would have been a pity because he was already looking forward to spending a little time with her.

She shook her head, but still didn't speak.

"Or perhaps you could take the financial loss and walk away before you invest any more."

Again she shook her head, and again she didn't speak.

"You put in everything you had into this venture, didn't you?" This time she nodded.

"Maybe it's a case of fraud. It was misrepresented by the agent who sold it to you and that's legal ground to get your money back."

"No," she whispered. "Not misrepresented."

Sam sighed. He knew desperation when he saw it, and he was seeing it. More than that, he knew what it would drive a person to do. It hadn't been so long ago he'd been desperate, too. Which was why he felt so compelled to help her through this, even though he knew he wasn't supposed to get that involved. In a couple weeks' time he'd have to deliver yet another blow—he'd have to write the report that would state something to the effect that this place was not suitable for a medical practice. As it existed at this very moment, it was not, and he doubted that Della had the means, let alone the where-withal, to accomplish the resurrection it would need. Which meant Della would be issued a cease and desist order from the state health commission.

Thinking about doing such a thing to her, even though he didn't know her, was already giving him a dull headache. Whatever that first blow was—the one that had brought her here looking so sad—it was devastating her, and taking a second blow on top of whatever the first had been seemed inevitable. Regrettable, but inevitable. He didn't even want to think about the expression on her face if that became the case.

"Why all the junk along the road?" she asked.

"Not junk. Sculpture. I understand it was an artists' colony years ago. Actually, Dr Bonn, who built this place, was an artist and he opened it up for people to come stay and create. That's why the medical facility is this far away from the village. It's an idyllic situation for an artist, not the town doctor."

"And I'm not an artist." She sighed wistfully. "So do you think the sheer isolation of it drove the subsequent doctors away?"

"I'm sure that had something to do with it. I think it has a certain appeal for someone who's newly graduated from medical school and looking for a start. But if you haven't lived an isolated kind of life before, it's probably pretty tough."

"So Dr Bonn, the artist…what happened to him?"

Sam looked up at a seagull flying overhead. It was heading to the water to find its next meal. Such a tough existence, always on the hunt to survive. That, he feared, was about to become Della's lot. "Someone in the village said he went to Paris to study art. The place ran down after that and nobody stayed long enough to fix it up." There had probably not been enough time under the health laws, and not enough interest considering the rough condition. Most of all, there was probably not enough potential for wealth. After all, weren't doctors supposed to be wealthy? According to his ex-wife, they were.

"And all that's left of the original art colony are those sculptures left behind? The ones on the road?"

"I don't know. I was out here earlier this morning to have a look, and this is all I've seen. The mayor told me there are some other buildings along the shore, old cabins where the artists stayed, but I didn't go out to have a look."

"It is amazing how a life can change. He came here to be a doctor and left here an artist. It's good he found what he really wanted." She looked over the knoll at the house. "Of course, what we want in life can change as much as life itself does."

"We all make mistakes, Della, but they don't have to ruin us." Empty words, he knew, but he felt like he should say something uplifting even though he wasn't the one who had got her into this mess. "If you do leave, I can't imagine that starting over should too difficult."

"This is my starting over. And you're wrong. It's very difficult. I've done it a lot lately and I don't want to do it again. This was supposed to be my last time."

Was she a lady with a past? If so, it couldn't have been much of a past since she was still allowed to practice medicine. He'd checked those credentials before she'd arrived and she was good in her licensing. "You know, I'm not sure what's going on here, and you don't have to tell me. I'm not the nosey sort who pries, but you're in a spot I don't think you can fix and I don't feel good about leaving you out here alone. So how about we go back to Mrs Hawkins's bed and breakfast? I'll pay for a couple of nights until you figure out what you're going to do next, and that way we can both get a good night's sleep. If you stay out here, you won't be getting one, and neither will I for leaving you alone without so much as a pillow."

"But you were prepared to leave me here when you thought I knew how this place was, weren't you?"

"That was different. If it was your choice to move in when it's in this condition, that's your business. Some people like it rugged. But you didn't know, and somehow I'm guessing it wouldn't have been your choice if you had known."

Instead of answering, Della opened the car door and climbed out. "It is what it is, and it was my choice," she said, quite dispiritedly. "I appreciate your concern, but there's no need for it. I'll just…fix it up. Since I'll be here all alone, I should have plenty of time for that. You wouldn't happen to know if I have electricity, or running water or indoor plumbing, would you?"

He doubted it, and he was also beginning to doubt she had common sense since she was refusing to budge from here. "Don't know. But I suppose that now you've convinced your-self to stay, we should have a good look around to make sure it's fit for living." Although judging from the condition of the exterior, he doubted that having a look would matter too much. This place was not suitable for patient care and unless Della was some kind of a miracle worker with a hammer and nails, he didn't see how it ever would be in the short amount of time before his report was due.

Unfortunately, in his mind, the report to shut her down here was already half written. He could do it tonight, then move on to another assignment if that's what he wanted to do.

But in his heart he couldn't do it. Not until he absolutely had to.

Taking a long, discouraging look at the bare bones of her new life, Della shuddered as she walked toward her house. It would have been pretty once. She could almost picture it a hundred years ago, all bright and new, with white wicker furniture on the porch, and ferns and begonias hanging from the ceiling. She could see herself sleeping there with Meghan on hot summer nights, or sitting on a porch swing, sipping lemonade with her in the late afternoon. So many wonderful things that could be if only the porch floor hadn't rotted a decade ago. But now the ravages of time and salty sea air had taken their toll. The house leaned a little, and the rusty tin roof that sloped down to cover the front porch sagged. All in all, it looked worn out, which was the way she'd felt so often lately.

Suddenly she felt sad for her little cottage on the beach. It had so much more potential than meeting this fate.

Della walked around the structure, spotting the chimney on the side of the house. Running her fingers over the brown stones it was made of, she noticed many of them were chopped away now. Even so, the prospect of a warm, toasty fireplace inside where she and Meghan could spend a long, chilly fall evening together, reading stories and toasting marshmallows, was so appealing that the thought of it nearly melted away all her anxieties. Nearly…because she'd have to have the windows put back in first. They were there, and the tiny, colonial panes made her think they were originals. But they had been removed from the house and were stacked in a pile near the chimney. The openings where they should have been were covered with dirty cracked plastic, as if someone had started a restoration, then stopped all too quickly. The last doctor? she wondered. Had he come here with optimism and ambition only to realize there was so much more to overcome than poor-fitting windows?

The yard was amazing, though. Della turned from the house to have a good look, and even with all the odd, deteriorating art on the way in, it was perfect. A place of hopes and dreams once. There were wispy trees along one stretch of her drive, a grassy knoll extending beyond her house and down the side opposite the tree lines, and out front a beautiful, unspoiled beach. Della sighed wistfully. She'd always wanted to live on a beach in Miami. Begged Anthony for it. Just a little cottage for the three of them where she could look out at the water. Instead, Anthony had bought a large, rambling deco home on a canal that was lined with other large deco homes, and docks jammed in together, board to board, for all the recreational boats that accompanied the houses. Then he'd bought the boat—one practically as large as this cottage—and lined up in that ostentatious weekend queue to take it out and show it off. The whole lifestyle there was so close and stifling, with all that togetherness, she would have happily traded it for breathing room with a view.

This was her breathing room with the view. Only problem was, it wasn't in the condition she needed. "Since you know my secret, that I bought it sight unseen, would you happen to know where the clinic is?" She was hoping it wasn't the barn she saw sitting back near the trees.

"It might be the barn. Or one of the guest cottages out there somewhere. But I haven't seen it."

"Well, wherever it's hiding, I hope it's in better shape than the house." If it wasn't it would have to be her first priority. Getting her patients into a fit establishment was more important than her own comfort. At least, until the time came when the judge would have a look at what she'd set up for her life with Meghan.

He smiled. "If it's got the same view as all this, I can understand why the artists came here. It's a perfect place to do a painting, or even write a novel, if you're a writer."

The last he said with a slight sigh, and she wondered if his heart might be in an art—painting or writing. Maybe even having a go at one of those junkyard sculptures. "With a view like this, I'm afraid the best I can ever do is enjoy a painting of it, or sit and read a book where I can take an occasional glance at it." Turning her attention to a wild guinea hen strutting off the front porch, Della watched it wander around to the back, stopping occasionally to peck at something in the dirt. Then she shut her eyes, hoping that when she opened them again the house would be something with green shrubs, red and yellow tulips in beds along the walkway, and a picket fence. When she opened them, though, everything was the same. Since, apparently, there wasn't a miracle to be performed, she wondered what came next.

As it turned out, Della didn't even have time to ponder that question before a pickup truck honked a greeting and came to a stop next to Sam's SUV. Immediately, half the town of Redcliffe hopped out. At least, to Della, it looked like half the town. It was actually the Brodsky family bringing all their kiddies for a check-up. Four of them plus Mom and Dad—Nola and Matt—both of whom also expressed the desire for a check-up. "Nothing's really wrong with any of us, except that Bianca has a little bit of a sore throat," Nola explained. "But since you're here, we thought we might as well be the first. And it will be so nice not to have to go to the mainland for this."

Bianca was two, and besides a sore throat she also had a slight fever, Della discovered when she saw the child's flushed cheeks.

"Is she cranky?" she asked, reaching over to take the toddler from her mother's arms.

"Quite. And nothing's calming her down."

"Is she eating?"

"Not much. She gets fussy when we try to feed her. Refuses to take it or spits it out when she does."

"I'm not really set up here to practice yet," she said, looking at Sam to see if he had a suggestion. He didn't, and he indicated as much with a vague shrug of his shoulders.

"I haven't even had time to go inside my…" She hesitated to call it her house, even though it was. Somehow, the image of a competent doctor didn't fit here, not on this property, not in this house, and as bad as things were, she really did want to get off to a good start. "My, um, building, here. I haven't unpacked yet."

"We'll be glad to wait," Nola offered. "And I'm sure Matt could take the other three and go play on your beach for a while, if you don't mind." The other three were Ryan, aged four, Keith, aged five, and Shawn, aged six. Brave woman!

For a moment, Della wondered how Nola could divide herself in so many ways, having that many young children to tend. At one time she'd thought about a brother or sister for Meghan, but Anthony had said no more children, then to emphasize his objection, had gone off and had a vasectomy. Another one or two besides Meghan would have been nice, though.

"I'll tell you what. Let me put Bianca down in the back of my car and have a look at her, then I'll set up appointments for the rest of you when I have things more settled here." When, or if.

Nola gave her a pleasant smile. "We didn't mean to impose, but when we heard you were here, we got so excited… It's hard raising children when there's not a doctor handy."

"What about emergency services?" Della asked, as she

cradled the toddler in her arms and walked over to her borrowed SUV.

"Helicopter if it's urgent. Boat if it's not." She laughed. "Pray that the weather is good when you have to go."

What a tough way to live a life, Della thought. Then she remembered this was the way she was going to live her life for the next five years. Apparently, you could either abide it or you couldn't. The last two doctors couldn't, and she was sure hoping she'd be the one who could. "Look, while I examine Bianca, why don't you go wait…" in the waiting room, except she didn't have one "…on the beach with your husband and sons? I'll call you over when I'm finished." She looked out to the beach as Matt and his boys waded out into the surf, hand in hand. It wasn't the most orthodox of waiting rooms but, on the bright side, it didn't require hundreds of dollars' worth of magazine subscriptions for the adults and toys for the children.

"You're going to treat that baby in the back of your car?" Sam asked, stepping over to observe once Nola had joined her family.

Sighing, Della said, "I have to treat her someplace, don't I?"

"You should have told them to take her to a hospital on the mainland until you're set up to practice here. That's what they've always done before."

Della kicked a piece of driftwood aside and laid Bianca down in the back of the SUV as Mayor Bruce Vargas pulled up in his truck and got out. "Except now that they have a doctor, they don't have to." She understood his concern, but he didn't understand her urgency. This was the first step. It wasn't a very big one, but it was a very necessary one. One patient at a time and she'd figure it out as she went. "These people know the condition of this place better than I do, and they're willing to come here to be treated regardless of it, so I'll find a way to treat them. It wouldn't be nice of me to turn them away." Especially since they had a heavy financial investment in her. "So I'll do the best I can for now."

She glanced up at the house on the knoll. Somehow, she would have to figure it out. And soon. "So, I have a medical bag in the back seat. Would you mind handing it to me?"

"You're really going to do this?"

"I'm really going to do this. Then afterwards I'm going to go have a look at the mayor's shoulder, like he asked, and if I'm lucky, somebody else might come along later."

"Oh, they'll come along all right. A doctor is a precious commodity, and they won't let her go to waste."

"She's teething," Della explained as she handed Bianca over to her mother. "Her gums are a little swollen and red, and her fever is elevated, but only a little. Nothing to worry about. Does she have diarrhea?" she asked.

Nola nodded. "My other three never went through this when they teethed."

Meghan had gone through it, too, frightfully so. She had been fussy off and on, and for weeks Anthony had slept in a hotel, claiming the crying kept him awake and he needed to be fresh for his surgeries. It had been a valid point, but in retrospect Della wondered if he'd been having an affair even back then, and using that as an excuse to sleep with someone else. "Some children do, some don't. Bianca is going to have a bit of a problem with it, I'm afraid."

"Does she need antibiotics?" Matt Brodsky asked.

"She doesn't appear to have an infection so, no. Antibiotics can be rough on young children, and taking them can start an immunity, which isn't good." Bianca wasn't congested in either lung, her eyes were bright and responsive, her respirations and pulse normal. Her tummy didn't hurt, her legs and arms moved normally. And the only time she whimpered was when Della ran a finger over her gums. In her opinion, the course of fewer medications was always the best when it could be managed. "Make sure you keep her off of dairy products for a week. Also, try to keep her quiet as much as you can keep a two-year-old quiet, and think about freezing some fruit juice and letting her suck on it. She'll love the taste and the cold will feel pleasant against her gums. The fluid will help keep her fever down, too. Just make sure the sharp edges of the frozen cube are rounded off."

She was good. Sam had to admit she was very good at this, and she had quite a way with the child. A natural. More than that, she loved it. That was so plain on her face, the way her eyes lit up, the way she smiled. For those moments when she'd been examining the little girl, Della had had the look of a woman who wasn't carrying the weight of so many troubles with her.

"How much do we owe you, Doc?" Matt asked, pulling his wallet from his pocket.

"One beach call?" She thought about it for a moment, then settled on an amount, quickly pocketing the bills when they were offered.

"That wasn't bad," she said to Sam as the Brodskys drove off. "And, believe it or not, that's the first time I've ever been paid for my services. Back in Miami, in the clinic, I received a weekly stipend. It's kind of fun, earning something for myself."

Such a simple thing, Sam thought. A small amount of money and she was thrilled over it. What kind of life was she coming from? And what in the world was he going to do about helping her in this new life? Helping her without losing his job?

Somehow, he couldn't fit the two together.

CHAPTER THREE

"WITHOUT tests I can't tell for sure, but I don't feel anything out of place—no tumors, no significant swelling," Della said as Mayor Vargas sat shirtless in the opened back of her SUV while she prodded and twisted his arm. Besides being tall, he had an extraordinary muscle mass, the evidence of a rigid, disciplined workout routine. "You've got full range of motion, which is good, and I'm not even feeling any popping, which is good, too. If you had an injury like a torn rotator cuff, you'd be experiencing some limited range."

"It comes and goes," he conceded. "Has been for months now, and just when I think it's bad enough to have it looked at, it gets better and it seems like a waste of time."

"Both shoulders?" she asked, switching her exam to his left shoulder. Manipulating her fingers along the shoulder line from his neck out to the furthest part of his shoulder, Della kneaded hard enough to assess the muscle, then she worked his entire arm up and down, back and forth, and at last in a wide circle.

"Not usually, but sometimes I get a twinge."

Next she went in for the final diagnosis and did a deep, pinpointed probe to the joint, one so hard that the mayor flinched. "Hurt a lot?" she asked.

"Like you knew exactly where the worst spot was and dug right in."

"I did." Della smiled. "Takes practice, and years of poking and prodding," she said as she returned to his right shoulder for the same pinpointed probe, which elicited both a flinch and a gasp from him. The mayor actually pulled away from her. "But along with the pain comes a diagnosis and a treatment plan."

"One that's good, I hope," he said, rubbing his sorest shoulder.

Della glanced over at Sam, who was sitting casually on a tree stump. This had been a simple exam, yet he was watching it very intently. Did he want to be back in practice again? On impulse, she asked, "Would you take a look, Sam?" She really didn't need his opinion. With or without tests, the mayor had bursitis. The symptoms fit, the pain response fit, and to be sure she'd send the mayor over to Connaught for a blood test and X-rays. But something was compelling her to include Sam in this, and she wasn't sure what it was. Maybe only a hunch that he wanted to be in practice, or a little wistfulness in his eyes.

"Um, sure," Sam responded quickly, then hurried through the knee-deep grass to the car. "I used to be an internist, so I think I can handle a second opinion."

He did much the same exam as she had, poking and prodding, and amazingly she caught herself almost transfixed, watching him work. Sam was so intense about it, so serious and methodical. And the wistfulness she'd seen in his eyes earlier turned to…was it passion? He might be a doctor she would trust Meghan's care to, and that was the highest praise she could give.

"Well, the bad news is…" he started.

Both Mayor Vargas and Della blinked in surprise.

"The bad news is that I'll never have your build, no matter how hard I work out. How many hours a day do you train?"

"Two, sometimes three. Weights, mostly. Some boxing, a little basketball, swimming."

"Like I said, that's the bad news...*for me*. The good news for you is that I'm going to concur with Dr Riordan's diagnosis."

"Which I haven't made," she reminded him.

"But you were going to say bursitis, weren't you?"

"Bursitis?" the mayor asked.

"Bursitis," she confirmed. "An inflammation of the bursa." Which he didn't know about, judging by the puzzled look on his face. "We all have hundreds of bursae throughout our bodies. They decrease the friction between two surfaces that move together, most commonly in areas such as where muscles and tendons glide over your bones. Think about a small plastic bag filled with a little oil. You can rub it between your hands and there's a smooth glide to it, but if you remove the oil it's a rather rough rub. Constricted. That's basically the function of the bursa, to provide that smooth rub, and if it becomes inflamed, it loses its glide. Hence, bursitis."

"And how did I cause that?"

"Repetitive motion over a long period of time is one way. Or an injury. I'm guessing it's from your workouts, though."

"Is it curable?"

"Not curable as much as it's manageable, but it does have a tendency to flare up from time to time, which means you may have to, at some point, adjust your workout routines to favor your condition. But we'll deal with that after I see the X-ray report. For now, I want you to massage your shoulder for about fifteen minutes with an ice pack, three or four times a day, and make sure you don't leave the ice on any spot for more than a few seconds or you can actually get frostbite in your muscle."

"Instead of an ice pack with regular ice cubes, freeze some water in a paper cup then roll that over your shoulder in a massage," Sam added. "Feels a lot better than ice cubes."

Della gave him an appreciative stare. "Voice of experience?"

"I fancied myself as a writer once. Sadly, I was one inflamed bursa away from writing a best-selling novel." He rubbed his elbow, then grinned. "Struck down in the middle of my prologue."

"You couldn't be a writer so you became a doctor? Aren't you quite the multi-faceted man?" Like the doctor who'd gone off to Paris to be an artist. So where was Sam's real heart? she wondered briefly. "Anyway," she said, turning back to the mayor, "take ibuprofen for a week. Go by the recommended dosage on the label, then come back and see me in a couple of days and we'll take a look at how you're getting along and figure out what to do from there. Also, by then I'll have found my prescription pad, and I'll write you a script for lab work and X-rays."

Her second appointment for the day now over with, Della received her pay with almost as much glee as she'd received her first. Glancing up at the gray clouds rolling in as she tucked it away in her pocket, she was hoping against hope her roof wasn't going to leak, because a patch was *not* the place she wanted her first earnings to go. Most of it would go for the clinic, but a little would buy Meghan a gift.

"Are you sure you're going to stay here with the storm coming in?" Sam asked. "I'm not sure about the condition of your house. It might leak."

"It looks like I'll be finding out in another few minutes," she said, heading up to the porch.

"Like I said before, I think that agent who sold you this practice should have been more honest about it. There may still be room to get out of the contract."

She stopped on the first step and looked at Sam. "He was honest. I simply didn't ask enough questions. And I should have come here first to have a look. But I didn't so it's all water under the bridge now." She glanced upward at the gray sky again, hoping there wasn't soon to be water in her kitchen, living room and bedroom, too. "Besides, I have real patients now, and it appears my practice has officially opened." All that was true, but it didn't make the situation any easier. Still, something could be worked out. It had to. That's the mindset she had to keep about her. For Meghan, she would make it work, or she'd be forced to return to Miami, contenting herself with a visit from her daughter on alternating weekends and holidays, while Anthony's parents raised her. With that in mind, there simply wasn't another choice here. "So, I'll stay and see how it goes."

Della reached into her pocket to feel the money folded in there. It was silly of her, but it felt good to be on her own. If the situation hadn't been so dire, it might have been laughable—the wife of Dr Anthony Riordan going almost giddy over a few dollars. She hoped that wherever he was now, heaven—which she doubted—or hell—which was likely the case—he had a lot more to fret over than money. "Guess it's time to take a look at the rest of my bad news." As she said that, a jagged streak of lightning split the sky, followed by an earsplitting roll of thunder. "It just keeps getting better, doesn't it?"

"We should make a run for it," Sam urged, grabbing Della's hand to pull her along with him toward the house, "before we get drenched. These storms pop up out of nowhere like that, and they can be pretty bad."

Della couldn't help herself. She yanked herself away from Sam and turned her face to the heavens. As the sky opened up and it began to pour, she stood in the middle of her falling-down-you'd-have-to-be-crazy-to-own-it calamity of a new life and laughed. It was either that or cry, and crying wasn't going to help her accomplish what she needed to here, because she needed to do so much in so little time.

* * *

Inside, in the kitchen, Sam opened and slammed shut every door and drawer, looking for matches. "You don't happen to smoke, do you?" he called to Della, who was huddled, soaking wet and shivering, on a stool in front of the unlit fireplace in the living room.

Too dumbfounded to comprehend everything around her, Della stared blankly at the room. It was empty and cold, and pelting raindrops on the roof sounded like gunshots exploding in rapid bursts, over and over. Outside, the dreary, late afternoon sky was turning darker by the minute, and since there was no electricity going, it was as dark inside as it was out.

Overall, it was dismal and Della simply sat in the middle of it, staring into the empty fireplace. "No matches," she called back. He knew she was trying hard to mask the discouragement in her voice, but he could hear it almost as well as he could hear his supervisor telling him not to get himself involved. But the sadness and near-desperation that slipped into her voice when her guard was down involved him.

"I don't smoke, but maybe we could use the lighter in the car," she continued. Adjusting her position on the stool, the floorboards creaked and groaned under the shift. "Want me to go get it?"

"What I want is for you to come to your senses. Go back with me to Mrs Hawkins's for the night and sort this thing out. You can take a shower, put on dry clothes, eat a fit meal, get a good night's sleep and have a fresh look at your options in the morning." She was so vulnerable, and yet so stubborn. He'd known her all of three hours and already he was feeling responsible and protective. Bad for his job, even worse for his personal life.

Once was enough. He'd learned that lesson well enough, and he sure wasn't willing to put himself through anything like that again. If he were being smart about this, he'd be on his way back to Mrs Hawkins's right now, to settle in for the evening. Alone! Without Della on his mind.

But it seemed he wasn't as smart as he'd thought he was, inasmuch as he wasn't heading out the door. More than that, he wasn't even thinking about heading out the door. Instead, he was already regretting the cold, hard floor on which he was about to spend the night if he couldn't convince her to return with him. Della wasn't about to be convinced, though. Deep down he knew that.

"No need to," she replied. "The roof doesn't leak, so I'll be fine."

"On the floor, in the dark. That's not fine, Della." It was more like insane. "What were you planning, anyway? To come here and find a quaint little seaside cottage all neat and tidy with everything you needed?"

"There's only one thing I need, and the rest of it doesn't matter. I've got furniture coming in a few days, I think I can be handy with some of the repairs and I've got a medical practice to organize. Sleeping on the floor in the dark isn't important." She stood up and walked over to the wall, then ran her fingers lightly over its covering. Layer upon layer of peeling wallpaper, highlighted by splotches of yellowed newsprint and dabs of peeling paint here and there. Solid, but ugly. "And I'll go have the electricity turned on tomorrow morning. So it's only for one night."

Sam stepped into the living room, holding up the matches he'd found in the back of one of the kitchen cabinets. "You're a stubborn woman, aren't you?"

She smiled. "I prefer to call it optimistic. Although my husband always accused me of being too stubborn for my own good. I think, though, I was too stubborn for *his* good. He wanted something I was too stubborn to be."

"Which was?"

She smiled at him. "Anything I wasn't."

"Divorced?" he asked.

She shook her head. "Widowed. Going on to four months now."

That took him off his guard. "I'm…um…I'm sorry, Della," he murmured, even though he didn't see much sadness on her face. He looked for it, too, but her expression seemed more relieved than sorry. The sadness he would have expected wasn't in her voice, either. Her pronouncement that she was a widow had come out as a rather flat statement, much the way he might make the same pronouncement of his divorce—sorry for the circumstance, but not totally consumed by it. So, had Della's marriage been as bad as his? "Is that why you're here, to get away from the memories?" Which was why he was there. That, and the fact that Massachusetts was almost as far away from California as you could get—California, where his ex-wife still roosted. That expanse of geography between them didn't hurt matters, either.

"Trust me, you can get away from a great many things, but the memories are something that will always stay with you. I'm here because I need a new life. It's as simple as that. Sometimes you have to go back to the beginning and start over to find the place you're meant to be. That's what I'm looking for—the place I'm meant to be."

"And you think you're meant to be here on Redcliffe?"

"It doesn't matter what I think. I'm here, I've bought this place and as of this afternoon my new life started. That's where optimism will help me more than being stubborn. I have a lot to do, and I'm going to have to look on the bright side in order to do it." She flicked off a piece of brittle wallpaper and watched it flutter to the bare wood floor. "Stubborn's what'll keep me going, though."

Maybe befriending a new widow put a little more of a

noble spin on his need to help her, but somehow Della didn't seem like a typical widow in mourning. She was mourning something, though, and it should have been her husband, but to Sam it seemed like there was more to it. Was there something deeper than the loss of a husband? "I suppose there's potential here," he said as he crossed over to the fireplace to start a fire. "You've got a sound structure, and that's always the best place to start. It's worthy of some optimism, too, because without it you do start from the beginning. With it, the course of what's to come is already outlined." He was starting again without that structure. The course of what was to come with him wasn't anywhere close to being plotted on an outline.

"An outline is good," she said. "It gives you direction and I've always been the kind of person who likes that. Heaven knows, I haven't always followed the right outline but, even so, you're correct. A sound structure is worthy of optimism."

He might have asked more questions, but he decided if she wanted to let him in, she'd have to be the one to open the door. The truth was, he wasn't sure he wanted her to do that. Being drawn to her was one thing, and he was. But being drawn in was something completely different. It came with an involvement he didn't want. He was barely involved in his own life and adding to that wouldn't work. Sam let out a discouraged sigh. "So since we're looking for something optimistic here, I say it's the stack of dry firewood next to the fireplace. Dry's better than wet."

Sam held up a single match, forcing a smile to his face. He didn't even like to think about the uncertainties in his own life, such as where he was going, what he would be doing when he got there. And look at him now, on the verge of spilling all that to Della. Out of sight, out of mind was the best way of avoidance. But Della struck a chord that almost compelled him straight to the confessional, and that was yet another reason to stay uninvolved. Bottom line—her need brought out a need in him that scared him to death. A rudderless man had no business connecting with that kind of an encumbrance. "One strike and we'll be all warm and toasty in a matter of minutes. Is that optimistic enough?"

"One match is very optimistic."

Or foolish, he thought. Because there was often a very thin line drawn between optimism and foolishness, and thinking that he could have a go at a real fire with one match was foolish. Thinking that he could be around Della and not get involved on some level was probably foolish, too. "So once I get this fire started, how optimistic should we be about finding something to cook over it?"

"I have granola bars," she said. "And a couple of bottles of water. I brought them on the airplane in case I got hungry."

He laughed. "Optimistically, that could make granola bar soup, but I've had my heart set on a nice juicy hamburger all day. Would you consider going back to the diner with me later, even if you're not going to spend the night at Mrs Hawkins's? Maybe we could scrounge you a blanket and a pillow somewhere along the way."

"I think I have dinner coming to my door later tonight."

"Ah, the ladies of Redcliffe," he said, trying to mask a bit of disappointment. Dinner was not an involvement. It was a necessity. At least, that's what he was telling himself tonight. Taking Della to dinner was a necessity, except it wasn't going to happen.

"The ladies of Redcliffe…you say that as if it's a bad thing."

The ruin of his date with Della was a bad thing, but maybe the ruin of his date with Della was also a good thing. The first mark on his outline. "Anybody who comes bearing food is a good thing, and I'm optimistic that if you ask me to stay for supper I'll eat my fair share of some very good home cooking."

"I don't get involved, Sam," she said, in all seriousness. "We can be colleagues, we might even become friends, but I do not get involved beyond that. What we have right here, right now is all it's going to be. And I'm not implying that you're working up to something, because you're probably not. But in all fairness, I did have to warn you. If that's acceptable, I'd love to have you stay for supper."

Words taken from his own mouth. They were in the same place when it came to involvement and that was a relief because he had an idea Della was going to be much more stubborn with him about maintaining the proper distance than he could ever be with her. "Are you always so forward?"

"No, but maybe if I had been in the past I wouldn't be in this mess now."

"Well, as a survivor of the divorce wars who has no intention of ever getting close to anything like that again…" He held out his hand to her. "Friends?"

Della smiled, and took the proffered hand. "Friends. And I'm sorry. Sometimes I get edgy about people's intentions. I know you're trying to be helpful, but the last people who said they wanted to help me stabbed me in the back."

"Is the knife out yet?"

"No, but I'm working on it. In the meantime, I'm glad you'll be staying. I don't have much of an appetite and the food the ladies will be bringing will spoil since I don't have an operating refrigerator yet." She frowned. "I haven't looked into the kitchen. Do I even have a refrigerator?"

"A very, *very* old one."

"And it will work," she said.

"Optimistically," he replied, as he bent to light the fire. Fourteen matches later, Sam stood up and backed away from the tiny spark that had finally caught. "Not bad for a beginner. A little long on matches and pathetically short on talent, but it'll catch."

"You've never done that before?"

"I'm from California. Southern part. Normally, we don't build fires with wood. We have those nice little fireplaces that operate off gas or electricity, where all you have to do is turn a switch, then instant fire."

"You're an awfully long way from home, aren't you?" she said, stepping closer to the heat, then kneeling down in front of it.

"Sometimes it doesn't seem like it's far enough," he muttered, taking care to keep his distance from her. Kneeling down there next to her to take in some of that heat would have been nice, but she would move away. That much was already clear about Dr Della Riordan. She would always move away.

"Is that the reason you're doing administrative work instead of practicing medicine?" she asked. "Something about the divorce wars?"

"Something like that." No need to tell her anything more. That way they could stay professional, detached, colleagues at a distance. Which was the way it was supposed to be. "So, how about I go bring in your bags? I think the rain has let up a little." He glanced out the plastic in place where the window should have been. It had slowed for now, but not for good. Della had a night full of storms to look forward to. That's the way these coastal weather fronts worked—one following on the heels of another.

She smiled, and for the first time he saw that undertow of worry diminish just the slightest. "I appreciate your help," she said, leaning in to warm her hands, "but you really don't have to treat me like I'm helpless because, in spite of appearances, I'm not."

"Just think of me as a friendly neighbor helping you move in."

"Except you're not a neighbor."

"But I'm friendly." He chuckled. "Look, I'll be right back. Is the car unlocked?"

Della took a look in the kitchen after Sam went to fetch her bags. It was a plain and basic room. One very old refrigerator, as he'd said, a wood stove she didn't have a clue how to use, and that was it. It looked sound enough, except for the peeling paint and the cracked linoleum, and with a little work… She sighed. Everything needed a little work. Instead of dwelling on exactly what that work would entail, Della wandered down the hall to the two bedrooms. Like the kitchen, the bones here were good, but the house lacked care. No one had loved it in a very long time. That was like her, wasn't it? No one had loved her in a very long time, either. Except Meghan. "Maybe I can make it work for us, Meghan," she whispered as she stood in the doorway of the smallest bedroom and imagined it painted in pink and purple.

Meghan loved pink and purple but, then, what five-year-old didn't? Two walls pink, two walls purple. Or maybe she could go half and half, with purple on the bottom and pink on the top. They'd find some kind of a pink and purple border to separate the two colors, and perhaps even paint her bedroom furniture pink and purple. Anthony's parents had bought it and it was solid maple. Brown and so boring for a little girl. A little splash of color would suit it beautifully.

Just making the plans for Meghan's room brought the tears back to Della's eyes. Had it been only that morning that she'd said goodbye? The judge had ordered the Riordans to allow visitation, but they'd been very grudging about bringing Meghan to the airport. In the end, they'd given in, then warned Della that missing her scheduled visits with her daughter wouldn't look good in the court record. Vivian had even suggested that Della leaving the state might be construed as abandonment. Of course, the Riordans wanted her to miss those visits, and they wanted it on the record that they'd spoken with her about the situation. It was so clear they didn't want her getting Meghan back—the crowning punishment for staying with their no-good son for as long as she had. "Which is why I've got to make this work for us, Meghan. I'm not abandoning you. I promise, I'm not abandoning you. Not ever."

Turning to look at the bedroom across the hall, Della couldn't envision anything there. That would be her room, but she couldn't dream past the faded orange and green flowered wallpaper and the plastic window. In that particular room there was nothing beyond drab, and she didn't care. Drab was fine as long as Meghan got her pinks and purples.

"Doctor?" a quiet voice queried.

Gasping, Della spun around to find a young girl standing in front of her. She was about sixteen, Della guessed, and nervous. "Can I help you?" she asked.

The girl nodded, but said nothing. Instead, she stared at the floor.

"Are you ill?" Della ventured.

She shrugged. "Maybe. But I don't know." She paused, looking back over her shoulder. "He's not coming in here, is he?"

"Who? Dr Montgomery?"

"If he is, maybe I can come back when he's not here."

"I can ask him to stay outside, if you'd like."

"Thank you," the girl said quietly.

Della dashed to the front door to stop Sam on his way back in. "I have a patient who doesn't want a man in the house," she whispered.

"A most delicate situation," he commented, giving her an understanding nod.

"At sixteen, everything's delicate."

He set her bags on the porch and stepped back from the door. "How about I go back to town and find you a blanket and pillow? When I return, with any luck the ladies will have brought supper out."

"Is there a pharmacy in town?"

He nodded.

"Could you bring me a home pregnancy test?"

He threw his hands into the air in surrender. "But we've only just met. I swear I didn't…"

She laughed. "And you won't." Pulling out the money she had tucked in her pocket, Della handed a twenty-dollar bill out the door to Sam, but he refused to take it.

"This one's on me," he said, trotting down the stairs. "But if any of the ladies bring pie, especially apple, I get your piece."

She faked a frown. "That's an awfully steep price to pay, don't you think? Especially when apple is my favorite."

"In that case, I might be persuaded to save you a bite or two." Sam tossed her a playful little wink along with a mischievous grin, then he was off. Della stayed on at the door and watched until the taillights of his SUV disappeared down the winding road, *her winding road*. Then she returned to her third patient of the day. As she grabbed up her medical bag and led the girl back out to the living room, she motioned for her to take a seat on the stool in front of the fire. "He's gone," she said. "So, first, before we do anything else, tell me your name."

"Gina, Dr Riordan. Gina Showalter."

"Call me Della." Dr Riordan sounded too much like her late husband, and the less she had to remind her of him, the better. She could have changed her name, of course, but for Meghan's sake she wanted to keep their names the same. There had already been too much upheaval in her daughter's young life and Della wasn't about to throw a little more of it onto the heap. "By the way, how old are you, Gina?"

"Almost seventeen," she replied, still very quiet.

"And you live here on Redcliffe?"

"On Bartlett Row. Number ten."

"Do your parents know you're here?" She was old enough to have confidentiality, but it was always nice to know the family situation.

"No, ma'am. I didn't tell them. But I'm able to pay you myself. I have a part-time job…"

Nodding, she pulled an old wooden crate over in front of Gina and sat down, ending up substantially lower than her patient and actually having to look up at her. Not the best of circumstances. None of this was, but so far none of her patients had objected "So why did you come to see me on a bad night like tonight, Gina?"

"I might be pregnant." She sniffled back a tear. "I didn't mean for it to happen but we…"

For starters, a serious talk on proper precautions was in order. For a moment, she thought about Meghan, wondering how that very sensitive mother-and-daughter talk would go when the time came. More than that, she wondered if she would be the one to have it with her daughter, or if the court would turn over all parental responsibilities to Meghan's grandmother for that sort of thing. "How long since your last period, Gina?" Della asked, trying to sound more like a friend than a doctor. If this girl was pregnant, there would be plenty of time to sound like a doctor in the future, and right now Gina really needed a friend.

"I don't keep track. Maybe a couple of months. But I'm not sure because I'm not always regular."

"So you may have missed two? Any possibility you've missed more than that?"

"I don't think so."

"And you haven't take a home pregnancy test?"

Gina's eyes flew wide open with that question, and her face turned completely white. "I couldn't. They would find out. Mr Delahanty at the pharmacy would say something if I bought one…or if we even bought condoms."

Now it was making sense. The talk of a small town was one of the drawbacks of a small town. Everybody knew what everybody else was doing. "Well, I'll need to do a pelvic exam at some point, but I'm not set up for that right now. So in the meantime I'd like to do a general exam to make sure you're in good health. Then tomorrow morning you can come back and take a pregnancy test, and if that's positive we'll figure out a way for the next part of the exam."

Poor girl was so frightened, Della's heart went out to her. She was awfully young to have so much commitment ahead of her. She was a bit thin, though, so maybe it was simply a hormonal imbalance come about because of her weight. Or perhaps the fear of a pregnancy had caused an imbalance or upset. Whatever the case, it was good that Gina had sought her out. Actually, it was nice that others had sought her out. It was a modest start, but nice.

Back in Miami, in the clinic, she was simply the next doctor in the queue, rarely ever seeing the same patient twice. While she loved the work, she missed the intimate contact, and this practice, if nothing else, was going to be all about the intimate contact. That left her with a good feeling as she did a cursory exam on Gina—blood pressure, pulse, breath sounds.

"Everything seems fine," she pronounced. "And like I said, I want to see you back in the morning for a pregnancy test."

"But what if I am, you know…what if I really am?"

It was too soon to talk options. She never did that until she knew for sure. "I want you to have a test first. When we know more we'll figure out what to do."

"My mom's going to kill me if I am." Gina said, as she pulled on her T-shirt and grabbed up her jacket.

At least Gina had her own mother around. Della hadn't been that fortunate for the last half of her own youth, and if she couldn't turn this into a real medical practice, Meghan would be without her mother for much longer than that. "I'm not going to allow that to happen," she whispered to herself as Gina headed out the door. "I'm not!"

CHAPTER FOUR

IT SEEMED like there were dozens of them, but in reality only ten women from the village had come calling, all bringing food. In Della's tiny house it simply seemed like many more, though, especially since some furniture had been brought out, too. As she looked over the vast array of casseroles, breads, salads, and, yes, three different pies spread about on the donated table, she felt overwhelmed by it all. These people were kind. They cared, and it seemed genuine.

She didn't remember all their names yet, but she did remember that the one with the flaming red hair was a schoolteacher and, when she had the chance, she meant to talk to her about schooling on the island. The short, roundish woman was the librarian, the taller, thin woman ran the grocery store, and the two ladies huddled into the corner, looking at the condition of the wallpaper, were stay-at-homes, she believed someone had said.

"It's probably too overwhelming to comprehend right now," a striking, auburn-haired woman close to Della's age said as she handed Della a paper cup of fruit punch. "New life, new job, all these people and your house in this condition. My name's Janice, by the way. Janice Newton. I own the art gallery down on Shoreline Way. One of many, but mine's the first one you see off the boat. Good location for the tourist trade we get here."

"Then you know all about *my* art collection?" Della asked, smiling. "The one outside?"

"A good idea neglected. Dr Bonn was the owner here, the one who built the house, and he had a vision to establish it as an art colony where struggling artists could come to create that great masterpiece. In theory it sounded good, but in reality Dr Bonn wanted to be one of them more than he wanted to be a doctor." She laughed. "The muse called, and he answered. What was meant to be an impressive garden museum got rather weedy, I think. Then the other doctors who followed him simply didn't like the life. From a distance it sounds good, but up close you've got to be the type for it, and they weren't."

"Did he make it?" Della asked. "Did Dr Bonn establish himself as an artist?"

"Actually, he did. His collections have been on display in several museums, and he's had some noteworthy commissions. I heard he's recently been commissioned to do a street sculpture in San Francisco, which is definitely considered establishing himself."

"Then it's good he listened to his muse."

"Something we'd all be better-off doing," Janice said. "So, do you have a muse, Della?"

"A calling. I like what I do, and I'm not going to run off to be an artist, or anything else. I was meant to be a doctor."

"Good, because we were meant to have a doctor and I'm glad it's you. People are already saying nice things."

"How long have you been here?" Della asked.

"All my life, off and on. I was raised here, then didn't return for a few years after I graduated from college. Eventually, when I realized what I really wanted in life, I knew I couldn't find it anyplace but here."

"So you came home." For someone who hadn't really had a place to call home since the age of fourteen, when her parents had been killed in a car accident, that did sound nice. Being tossed from aunt to uncle to distant cousin, then eventually landing in Miami with Anthony, Della had never really had the feeling that any one place was different from the next, and she wanted more than that for Meghan.

"Speaking of which, do you really intend on calling *this place* home right now? Molly Gentry over there is a Realtor, and maybe she can find you something better to rent, at least until you can get it fixed up."

A rental would be nice, but too costly. Besides, she needed to make a decent home for Meghan. It was what connected her when the threads seemed very tenuous. "I think this place has a certain rustic charm to it," she replied, smiling. "Thanks, but I'll be fine."

"We were actually surprised you accepted."

"It was a generous offer," Della said. "Hard to refuse."

Janice laughed. "Generous, if not dilapidated. The previous owner has been trying to sell it for so long and, taking a financial loss on it all those years, he refused to put any money into upkeep. The owner before that was much the same way, so your little house has seen years of neglect."

"And tomorrow morning, first thing, I'm going to the hardware store to see what I can find to start the repairs." She liked Janice. She was honest and to the point. It had been so long since she'd had any real friends outside Anthony's social circle, Della was, all of a sudden, looking forward to having a friend of her own—someone who didn't put on a pretense for the wife of the great Dr Anthony Riordan. An identity of her own, and a friend of her own—those were nice surprises she hadn't expected. "Starting with a home repair book."

"Sharon Farnham is the librarian. Just tell her what you need."

It was nearly an hour into dinner before Sam returned, and by the time he wandered in the door, Della had chatted with every one of the Redcliffe women in her living room. Three had made definite appointments over the next couple days, two had said they'd stop in with a child and one had made an appointment for her husband. Della was sure the effect of having a new doctor was much the same as having a new flavor of soda on the market—everybody rushed to try it right off, then the flurry died down when the new flavor settled into oldness. While she was still the new flavor, she would see as many patients as wanted to be seen and, with luck, establish herself well enough that the fast rush, when it settled, would still be regular.

"Save me some pie?" Sam asked, as he stepped into the living room with an armload of bedding.

"Do I look like the sort who would go back on her word?"

"When it comes to apple pie, you never can tell."

"Well, trust me, Doctor. I snatched it away from Thelma Rittenour's covetous eye, boxed it up all safe and proper for you, and you can either eat it here or take it home later." She smiled. "When Thelma's not watching."

"Except I'm not going back," he said, taking care to lower his voice so as not to be overheard. "I've decided to stay here tonight, whether or not Thelma Rittenour's still after my pie."

"I told you that I don't need you here," she snapped.

"No, I suppose you don't. But it's not going to be easy." He shoved the load of bedding into her arms. "And until you have a phone and electricity…"

"You're going to make it easier on me somehow by staying? If that's what you intend on doing, I don't want it, Sam. I'm fine. I can take care of myself." She didn't want to sound peevish, but she felt it. All those years of being told what to do, and it felt like she was right back there again, being choked into something she simply didn't want.

"You don't even know your way back to town."

"No need to tonight. As soon as everybody leaves, I'm going to bed." She looked at the spot on the floor in front of the fire. A little dusty and very hard, even with the bedding he'd brought, but that was only until morning. Then she'd make another plan for the next night, and a plan for the night after that until all the pieces came together in a complete picture.

"And what if you need a bathroom?"

She gave him a tight little smile. "I'm resourceful. And I don't need a cup of coffee to get me going in the morning, so I'm fine."

"Fine *and* stubborn."

"If that's what it takes to get me through, then, yes, I'm stubborn." It felt good, too. Previously she'd always been compliant. Apparently, much too compliant, considering the way things had turned out. Nobody was ever going to have that kind of control over her again. "Look, Sam. I appreciate what you're trying to do, but I don't need someone to take care of me, I don't need someone to protect me from the ghosties and ghoulies and long-legged beasties…" And things that went bump in the night. Della swallowed back a hard lump. Every night before Meghan went to bed they would check the closet together, then get down on their knees and look under the bed. After that, Meghan would beg her to say the ghosties poem.

Was Vivian doing that with Meghan tonight? Somehow, Della doubted that, and as she thought about Meghan crawling into that vast king-sized bed in the sterile Riordan guest bedroom, all alone and without her ghosties poem, the tears welled behind her eyes. Spinning around, Della practically ran down the hall into the room she would paint pink and purple, shut the door, and there, standing in the middle of the dirty, empty room, she let the tears stream down her cheeks, wondering how there could be any left since she'd already cried so many of them.

She hadn't lived with Meghan the past month, but she'd been close by and at night she would sit in front of the Riordan mansion until the lights in the guest room were turned off and say the ghosties poem to herself, for Meghan. She'd watched her daughter on the playground at kindergarten, been there to see her take a morning walk with her grandfather, and she'd had her court-approved visits. For a whole month, if there had been a possibility to have even a glance at her daughter, she had been in the position where she'd been able to, sometimes waiting hours.

But now...

Opening her eyes and swiping at the tears, Della's sight was beginning to adjust to the dark, and she could see where Meghan's bed would go. And her dresser and her dressing-table. She turned around, looking at the corner near the window. That would be a wonderful place to hang a net in which to keep her stuffed toys. Then her little table and chairs would go under the window. They could sit there together and have tea, and maybe plant a little garden outside the window for a lovely view.

"Della?"

Sam's voice broke the mood, and she pulled up the hem of her T-shirt to wipe her eyes. "I'm fine," she said, her voice a bit too wobbly to sound fine. "Just tired." That much was true.

"The ladies are leaving. I told them you're exhausted." He pushed the door open a crack. "Janice is taking most of the food, and she said she'll bring the leftovers back tomorrow in a couple of coolers."

"Thank you," she whispered.

"And Sharon, I can't remember her last name, said she'd have a stack of home-repair books ready for you at the library tomorrow. Someone else who owns the grocery will gather up some cleaning supplies if you want to stop by for them in the morning."

"I appreciate everything," she said. "But it's not your job to help with my personal life, and we don't know each other well enough for you to be involved in it."

"I don't want to sleep with you, Della, if that's what you're afraid of. I'm not some kind of lech horning in on a widow's grief, hoping to take advantage. And, no, I don't know you well enough to be involved with you in any way, but we do share a common bond, and I thought we might eventually become friends. But I'm not going to beg for it. Like it or not, you're going to be stuck with me for the next couple of weeks while you set up your medical practice because that's my job. But you don't have to worry. I'll keep it strictly professional."

With that, he walked away and Della listened to his footsteps echo through the empty house until they were gone. Then she was alone…alone in a dark, dirty, neglected house, fighting desperately to cling to her single hope. "Well, it's what you asked for," she said as she wandered back out to the living room. "You asked for it, and you got it." Sam had laid the bedding out in front of the fire. Pillows and blankets, and… She saw a plate sitting on top of the stool. Two bites of apple pie on it. "Why would I have ever been attracted to someone like Anthony?" she whispered, as she dropped down onto the blankets and reached for the bites of pie. Unlike Anthony, Sam was genuine. She thought he would be good with Meghan. Anthony had been neither—not genuine, not good with Meghan.

"Not good at all," she said, with a heavy sigh as she settled down into the blankets, hoping the fire lasted the night. The room had an early autumn chill to it, and the rain outside only accented what she was feeling inside. Empty. Totally, pathetically empty. "But I'm going to make this right for us, Meghan. I promise I will."

Della fluffed a pillow and pulled a blanket up over her, then turned to watch the sparks from the fire. She wasn't sure she would sleep, but somehow, being in front of the fire, with its cozy crackling and popping, didn't make her feel quite so alone. So she shut her eyes to enjoy the warmth and listen…

"Della!" Sam pounded his way up the steps and straight into the house without knocking. "Part of the road's washed out, and there's been an accident."

She bolted straight up. "I'll get my bag." Then, within seconds, she was halfway down the steps outside, following Sam in the rain. "How many cars?"

"Just one, but there were three passengers. Car's overturned. We've got help coming out from the village and they've radioed ahead to put the helicopter on standby for a run to the hospital in Connaught."

The wind was whipping around badly now, and the rain was coming down in sheets. As Della climbed her way over the knoll, her feet slipped out from under her and she fell then slid on her backside almost all the way down the other side. By the time she came to a stop, Sam was there, offering her a hand to help her up. "Do you know who's in the car?" she asked, almost holding her breath for fear it might be some of the ladies who'd come there this evening.

"Kids, I think. According to the sheriff, they like to come out here and do some off-roading when it's muddy. That stretch of road is rarely ever used because it winds around more than the other."

Della picked up her muddy medical bag and headed to her purple car, but Sam grabbed her. "Ride with me," he said, and it wasn't an invitation. "The road's a total washout and your car won't make it through." For once she wasn't going to argue, and in another half-minute they were on their way to the accident site. "Did you see it happen?" she asked, brushing the wet hair from her face.

"No, the sheriff hailed me as I turned onto the highway. Another group of kids saw it happen."

"Have you been to the site?" she asked.

"No, I came to get you. It's your medical turf. You need to be the one to call the shots."

"Look, Sam. About what happened earlier…everything that I said…"

"No need to explain."

"But there is. I was way out of line. You were trying to be nice and I was being…well, grumpy is a mild word for it, I think. I'm sorry, though. This whole transition in my life hasn't been easy, and I haven't started it the way I probably should have." She wouldn't tell him about Meghan. No need. That was her own private grief, and something she wouldn't share with anyone. Besides, how could you tell someone that the person who was about to care for the medical needs of an entire island had been deemed unfit to care for the needs of her own child? If ever there was a reason for the people here to refuse her services, that was it, and she knew exactly what the Riordans, and the judge, would do with that piece of information.

"You're still grieving the loss," he said sympathetically.

That much was true. But it wasn't Anthony's loss she was grieving now. She had grieved him, but not as a devoted wife should, and not the way a mother grieved the loss of her child—the way she grieved for Meghan.

"And I shouldn't have come on so strong," he continued. "I'm sorry, too. I simply assumed that…well, let's just say that if I'd found myself in your rather difficult position, I'd be begging for all the help I could get to straighten it out."

"You were trying to be a friend. There's no need to apologize, and if the situation were reversed, I'd probably do the same. Sometimes it's easier to give help than to receive it." Because receiving it came with an implied trust she wasn't ready to accept yet.

The vehicle hit a large hole in the road and if not for the fact that Della was wearing her seat belt, she would have bumped right out of the seat. "Sorry about that," Sam said, swerving to avoid a small tree off to the side. "Didn't mean for the things that go bump in the night to be you." He chuckled. "Or me."

Della gasped over the reference but didn't say a word.

"You know, ghoulies and ghosties and…"

"Ghosties and ghoulies," she snapped. "If you're going to recite it, then recite it correctly."

Sam gave her a sideways glace, but didn't say another word until they were at the crash site and out of the car. "It doesn't look like anybody's gotten out so far," he said, looking down the ravine at the overturned vehicle.

"You're right," she agreed, following him across the ridge to the post where the sheriff was waiting for them. "I need to get down there. And I'm sorry about snapping at you again."

He chuckled. "I'll have to admit, I've been snapped at for a great many things in my life, but never for my poetry recitation."

"I'm tired," she said. "It's no excuse, and I'm sorry." She smiled. "And I'm sorry again."

"For what?"

"At the rate I'm going, I'll owe you at least one more apology before the night's over, so I'm offering it in advance." She turned to the sheriff, who was illuminated in the beams of his patrol car. "Any sign of life?" Della called to him over the noise of the beating rain. He was an older man, a little round, and he made no move to indicate he wanted to do the heroics here. In fact, he seemed perfectly glad to lean back against his car and let the water roll off his plastic rain poncho. Of course, she didn't blame him. Getting down there wasn't going to be easy, and if he'd had a try, he'd have likely ended up being the fourth casualty out here.

"No, ma'am. I've called out, but no one answers. I've got the fire department on its way to help get them out of there, and some volunteers from town coming along, too. I figure we're going to need all the help we can get to hoist them up."

She look at Sam. "We can't wait," she said.

He nodded his agreement. Then, without another word between them, they went to the edge of the ravine together and looked down again. "I'm going to get my car turned so we can have light," he said, then he went back over to the sheriff. "You pull your car in closer, too."

In less than a minute the accident scene was lit up, and Della got her first good look at the scope of it. The vehicle was not only turned upside down, it had smashed into a tree. Hard impact, from what she could tell, and the front was folded in like an accordion. "I'll take the left side," she said to Sam, as she took her first step down the muddy, steep incline. Her footing gave way and she slid but didn't collapse into the mud.

Sam grabbed her from behind to steady her, and they balanced each other on the thirty-meter descent, both of them alternately slipping and stumbling and clinging to one another to keep from falling. It was more like one long slide to the bottom, and Della discovered as they reached the car that they weren't really at the bottom. The ravine leveled slightly there, but took another dip beyond the wrecked car and continued on for almost as far as they'd already come. "Hello!" she called as she grabbed hold of the car and pulled herself along to the side of it. "Anybody awake?"

No answer.

Sam reached his side first and looked in. "I see two," he called. They weren't fastened in apparently, because they were lying in a heap together on the interior roof of the car. "Driver's missing," he yelled, bending down in the mud and reaching in through the broken window to have a feel at a pulse.

On the opposite side, Della did the same. But she didn't have to reach so far because the boy on her side was close to the window, and she could feel the tiny shards of glass embedded in his skin as she slid her fingers over his neck to check for his pulse. He groaned before she found it, which answered that question. "Mine's alive," she shouted.

"Mine is, too, but his pulse is thready. And I've got lots of blood. He's wedged in pretty good, and I'm too large to get in to have a better look."

"I'm not," she shouted. Being barely five feet tall and weighing barely a hundred pounds didn't often have an advantage, but this time it surely did. Della slid her medical bag inside the car, then pulled herself around to Sam's position to have a look. "My guy over there's blocking the window, but I think I can have a go from this side. Think we can get the door open?"

"Rear door, maybe," he said, having a tug on the handle. It was stuck, but a couple hard attempts pulled it back enough for Della to slip inside.

"Never done anything like this," she shouted back to Sam as she slid on her belly across the interior car roof to the boy he'd already examined. It was dark in there, save for the car dome light that was flickering off and on, trying to decide if it wanted to stay lit or burn out. "Call up to the sheriff and tell him I need a couple of flashlights," she said, as she pulled her medical bag over and found her tiny penlight in it. "Tell him we're going to need an airlift and some way to get these boys out of here. And tell him we've only got two, that if there was a third, he's been thrown clear." She pointed her penlight forward, and stared for a second, shuddering at the sight. "Right through the windshield."

In the far-off distance, Della could hear the faint wail of a siren. It wasn't a fit night to be out, and she desperately wished these boys had taken heed of that. But at their age life wasn't about forethought. It was about the immediacy of the moment. And this moment was going to come with a dear cost for them.

"Sheriff said there were definitely three in the car," Sam said, handing a flashlight in to Della. "Can you tell what's going on yet?"

Della did a quick body scan. "Can't find any overt bleeding outside a few lacerations. But his pulse is weak and thready, and I haven't been able to maneuver myself into the right angle yet to get his blood pressure. How about yours?"

"Semi-conscious. Other than that, I haven't had a good look yet, and he's so large I'm not sure I can wedge myself in well enough to do much until we get him out of there."

As Sam slipped and slid back to the opposite side of the vehicle, Della pulled her blood-pressure cuff from her bag and wrapped it around her patient's arm. She put her stethoscope in her ears then inflated the cuff, after which she let the air out slowly. His pulse was so weak she could barely hear… Frowning, she re-inflated the cuff, repeating the procedure. "Palpable at forty," she finally said. Meaning it was danger-ously low. "Respirations are rapid, shallow…" She stretched forward to have a listen to his chest, then crawled around to assess his pupillary reaction. "Normal," she said, which really didn't mean anything is this case because she suspected a belly wound, and a prod of his belly, which was very rigid, told her he had an internal bleed going on.

"Any luck over there?" she called to Sam as she wiggled back up to her patient's head, trying to figure a way to stabilize his neck.

"In and out. He has a pretty good gash on his head and I can't get in past his chest. I'm a little concerned about the way he's wedged into all the broken glass, though. If he should start thrashing about…"

Della tossed Sam the stethoscope and blood-pressure cuff. "I think I've got an *in extremis* here," she whispered, even though if the boy could hear, he wouldn't know what that meant. Which was on purpose because it meant death within minutes if help didn't arrive soon. Even with help, she feared there wasn't much time to get him to a hospital and stop the internal bleeding. "Do we know how long ago this happened?" She held her breath for the answer, because she knew it couldn't be good.

"The sheriff estimated about ten minutes from the time he stopped me, which makes that about thirty minutes now."

Della shut her eyes for a moment to steady herself, then bent to the boy's ear. "Hi," she whispered. "My name's Della, and I'm a doctor. We're taking good care of you, and as soon as we get a few more people here to help carry you out, we're going to take you to the hospital. So you hold on for a little while longer. We'll get you some medicine and fix you right up." For all her carrying on about optimism earlier, there was very little of it in supply for this boy, and she gritted her teeth and held her breath as she felt his pulse again. Weaker, as she'd suspected. "Just another few minutes," she whispered.

* * *

Sam's big ox of a patient seemed no worse for wear. His vital signs were good, he didn't have a rigid belly or other evidence of an internal bleed, and he did regain consciousness every now and then for a few seconds. "We'll get yours out first," he said, as the firefighters slid their way down to the car.

"Tell them to look for the third one," she said, as she maneuvered the cervical collar one of the firefighters had brought down with him onto her patient's neck.

They were shining more light for them now, and Sam was able to watch her. She was hunched on her knees, crouched into such a tight ball he wondered how she could even move, let alone work, but she put the collar on the boy so easily he had to stop and admire it. These were horrible conditions and her patient was slipping away, but she worked with efficiency, trying to secure him for transport, that he thought she was one of the most skillful emergency workers he'd ever seen. Doctors like Della Riordan were rare. As bad as all this was, he actually liked working with her.

"Oxygen," she said, then reached out for the mask and tubing. "And I'm going to have to get him on a backboard somehow before we move him out of here. I need to start an IV, too. You wouldn't happen to have a catheter handy?"

"No, ma'am," the firefighter called in. "We're not paramedics."

"What's the ETA on the airlift?"

"There was a slight break in the weather, so they've landed now. But it's a mile down the road."

"Then let's put this young man on a backboard and get him ready for them. Radio them that I want an IV set up, normal saline for starters, and have an intubation kit ready just in case. I'll need him on a heart monitor, and have them call ahead to let the hospital know he's going straight to surgery."

"Yes, ma'am."

Amazing, Sam thought. She was absolutely amazing.

"Sam," she called, "can you help me with the backboard from over there? I know it's a tight fit, but if you could lean in a little further and hold my patient while I roll him forward…"

"Bart," Sam's patient mumbled. "He's Bart Talmadge. I'm Aaron Landers. Do you know where my brother is?"

"Your brother?" Sam asked, as he squeezed in past Aaron with his shoulder, but not enough to be of any help to Della.

"Marty," he gasped.

"He's already out of the car," Della said. "And as soon as we get Bart out, you'll be next."

"I'm coming over there," Sam said, but Aaron reached out and grabbed his hand.

"Don't leave me here," he sobbed. "Please, don't leave me."

"I'm fine," Della said, then she smiled across at Sam. "I really am."

He gave her a knowledgable nod. She really was fine, in more ways than he would have ever suspected, especially for someone who'd bought a brand-new life sight unseen.

CHAPTER FIVE

"CAN you move a little to the left, Doc?" the fireman outside the car shouted. The rain was coming down harder now. Various people were slipping and sliding up and down the ravine, trying to bring her the equipment she needed, as well as attempting to tie off the crumpled car so one gust of wind or one off-balance move didn't send it sliding even further down. "I can't get the backboard in the opening unless you can move over to the left."

Bart was ready to transport. Now it was a matter of doing it, which wasn't all that easy. She was already jammed in there so tightly she could barely breathe, and there was simply no place else to go. "Sam" she grunted, still trying to find that extra spot in which to wedge herself, "are you OK over there to get Aaron out? We need to do that first."

"I think they're going to have to do some cutting," he called. "I've got him propped so the broken glass won't cut him, but if he moves he's going to injure himself, maybe even cut through an artery…and right now with the way he's wedged in it's risky in the area of his femoral." The major groin artery. "I honestly think they're going to have to cut the door away before we do anything else."

"I'm running out of time over here," she shouted back, the frantic fear of actually losing her patient beginning to show.

Sam surveyed his options, which were few: Force Aaron through the opening and risk hurting him further, or wait, which meant sure death for Bart. "I might have a way," he finally said, "if you could get yourself into a position to support his legs."

"I can do that." Being able to twist around like a pretzel would have helped here, but since she couldn't do that, she scrunched into a ball and rolled over until her face was practically pressed into Aaron's feet. "Tell me what to do."

"How much can you wedge yourself under him?"

She assessed the situation. "Some. Enough to take off some of the weight."

"Then do it. When I give you the go-ahead, get yourself under him and lift up as much weight as you can without actually moving his body too far up."

She wasn't sure what Sam was going to do, but when he yelled his OK, Della slid her shoulder in under Aaron's feet to balance the weight. Pretty soon she felt a little less of his weight on her. It took several seconds before she realized that he was being pulled forward, and while she couldn't see the progress, she could hear the distinct grunts coming from the several people she assumed to be pulling the boy.

Aaron was very quiet through the process, and as his body moved on, she stayed underneath his legs as much as she could until she was practically at the car window in which he'd been lodged. Then, suddenly, he was out.

Della rose up and took a look, and saw a flurry of activity on the ground—strapping the boy to a backboard, trying to shield him from the rain, tying the board off to use a pulley to get it up the slope. "Sam," she called, but she didn't see him. He was probably in the thick of the activity, trying to secure his patient.

Quickly, Della crawled back over to Bart, then pulled the

backboard inside. Within seconds, she had him secured. "Get him out," she yelled, then took her place at his head, as the firefighters pulled him out feet first. When he was fully outside the wrecked vehicle, the same flurry of activity swooped in over him, and within seconds he was on his way up the ravine to the fire truck and the flight paramedics who'd come to help. Bart was in their hands now—they had the equipment to support him and the means to get him to the hospital.

Her part in this was over as far as Bart was concerned, and now she had another patient to help.

As the rain began to slacken, Della stood next to the car, looking for Sam, looking for signs of the third boy, looking at the full response of so many people from the village. Floodlights had been brought to the site, more car lights were aimed at the ravine, people with hand-held torches were flanking the sides of the drop-off, shining their lights down on the scene. There must have been a hundred responders of some sort up top now. The word had gone out and the people had come.

"Sam," she shouted. Where was he? Grabbing hold of the car, Della pulled her way over the mud slide to the far side of the vehicle but she didn't see him. "Sam!"

"He went down to the other fellow," one of the men called out to her. "And the doc's going to need some patching himself. He wedged himself in there against the car when they were pulling the kid out. Got under him to hold him up and act as a buffer to protect him from all the broken glass and metal shards sticking out. He took a few good cuts doing it."

Of course he would have, Della thought. He was the type who wouldn't even think about the danger to himself if someone needed help. Not like Anthony, who had winced over a hangnail. She looked further down the ravine. "You said he's down there?" she asked.

"Probably another fifteen meters. And it's awfully steep—

much more than it is up here. Watch yourself if you're going down."

Watch herself, indeed. Della assessed the slope, and figured she'd most likely slide down on her backside after a step or two. To her amazement, as she sidestepped into her ascent, one cautious foot over the other, she stayed upright. It was an infinitely long, slow journey through the mud and fighting the wind blowing at her back, trying to topple her over. Even with the lights shining down, there was practically no visibility, owing to the rain beating down so hard once again she was driven to ducking her head to avoid the sting of it on her face.

Nearing the end of her descent, though, when she finally looked up to see the hive of activity above, she paused long enough to regain her bearings, and as she did so a gust caught her off guard, sending her down the slope in an uncontrolled run, like a downhill skier picking up momentum and speed. She wasn't exactly sliding, but not exactly running, either, and the further her descent, the faster she went. Then suddenly she stopped, right in Sam's arms. But it wasn't a graceful stop. There was nothing pretty about it and it wasn't one where she might look up into his eyes when it was over and laugh. Rather, it was a hard slam straight into a broad chest, a slam that sent him over backwards and landed her on top of him. For a moment she heard ringing in her ears, felt her breaths coming tentatively. And she felt him underneath, but couldn't focus enough to see him.

It took about thirty seconds for Della to regain her wits, then immediately she gasped, "Sam, are you OK?"

"OK," he grunted, his breaths coming in more of a wheeze than a natural sound. "As soon as you get off me."

It was darker down here, but even in the dimness she could see the cut on his forehead at his hair line. It was bleeding, and caked with mud. "How is he?" Della asked, rolling off Sam into the mud. "The boy?"

Sam took in a deep breath then let it out slowly, coughed a couple times, then answered. "Won't be driving anything but a wheelchair for a few months. Both legs broken, broken arm, maybe a shoulder. Couldn't get in there to see anything else."

She sat up and started to push herself to her feet. "But he's OK?"

"For someone who's been through what he has, he's better than he should be." He finally sat up, then clutched at his ribs. "They're strapping him up and as soon as they can get him out of the bush he's lodged in, I'll splint him then send him up to the paramedics." He coughed again, then doubled over in pain.

"Are you *sure* you're OK?" she gasped, dropping immediately to her knees. She grabbed her penlight out to take a look at his head injury, but he shoved her hand away.

"Just dandy for someone who doesn't practice medicine." Sam took in a deep, ragged breath then forced himself to his feet. "Coming?" he asked. Instead of offering a hand to help her up, he wrapped both his arms around his middle. "Sorry I can't do the gentlemanly thing here, but it seems you busted some of my ribs."

"No!" she choked, not sure what to say. "Are you sure?"

"Sure," he said. "Played soccer in college. It's not the first time."

"Sam, I'm so sorry…"

He flagged her off with the wave of his hand. "Not a big deal. They'll heal."

"Or they'll perforate your lung if you fall, trying to get yourself out of here. So lie back down," she ordered, looking around for a spot that wasn't quite so exposed to the storm. "I'll have them send down a backboard."

"Don't need it," he grunted.

"You do need it, and you need some stitches as well. I'm taking you out of this rescue, Doctor. Until I've had a better look at you, you're not part of it. So go sit down over there." She pointed to a little break of bushes that might offer him some protection. "And don't get up until I tell you to." Instead of waiting for Sam to argue with her, Della ducked down the path to have a look at Marty Lander. Sam had been correct about his preliminary diagnosis. One broken tibia for sure, one broken fibula most likely—neither of which were compound fractures, which was good. Also, he had a shattered ulna mangled at such an angle she knew he'd need immediate surgery. As for the scapula, it was in a bit of a twist, too, but his other injuries prevented a good look. His belly wasn't rigid, though, and his pupils were equal and reactive to light. He was actually tracking the tiny beam of light as she moved it back and forth. Probably no substantial head injury present.

"Where else do you hurt?" she asked the boy.

"Everywhere," he said. Then he gave her a weak smile. "How's my car?"

"Worse than you are. It won't recover, but you will." She laughed. Typical teenage boy, thinking about the car first.

"The other doc said Bart and Aaron are OK," he said. "Did you see them?"

"I saw them and they're on their way to the hospital now." She hedged a bit here, because until he was stabilized she didn't want him worrying about his friends, and she especially didn't want him to know that Bart's condition was extremely critical. "Which is where you're going as soon as we can get you free from the bushes."

"We've got the chainsaw," someone yelled.

Martin's eyes went wide with fright, and Della gave his hand a gentle squeeze. Poor kid probably thought the worst— a field amputation of some sort. "For the shrubs. We can't get you through them until we cut them away."

"Can I have something for the pain?" he asked.

Truth was, she didn't carry medication with her. Not ever. And she hadn't been on the island sufficiently long to get any. "They'll give you something for the pain once you're on the helicopter."

Instead of waiting to get him out of the thicket to splint him, Della removed her rain slicker, pulled a pair of scissors from her bag, and cut several strips off the bottom of it. Then she wrapped the remainder about Marty's arm, and secured it with the cut-off strips. In her opinion, that was the least stable of his fractures and the one most in need of immediate care.

"We're going to cut now, Doc," one of the men yelled. "Don't move."

Don't move. Like she could. The only way she could move was down, which was exactly what she did. Della leaned over her patient and waited until the ear-splitting scream of the saws stopped, then she stood up and waved to the firefighters, who tied off the backboard and were waiting to pull it out. At her signal, several other men stepped in around her and grabbed hold of the board, then lifted it carefully off the ground. Again, a makeshift pulley device unfolded and Marty was hoisted up the slippery, muddy side of the ravine.

"Ready to go?" she called, trudging back over to Sam. "Because as soon as they get him up, they're going to send it back down for you."

"I can walk," he snapped, struggling to his feet.

"Well, if you do, you should know that I've got the chest tube to insert and the scalpel handy to make the cut between your ribs if you tear your lung with a rib edge, which is a distinct possibility here. But bear in mind I don't have any anesthetic yet, no bullet to bite, either, so it's going to be a raw cut. If you still want to risk all that by walking…"

"Lousy bedside manner," he muttered. "The doctor breaks my ribs then threatens me with a scalpel when I try to get away from her."

"But you can't get away, Sam. I know that, and you know that. So who's the one being stubborn now?" She tucked herself back in under the stand of bushes and sat down with him to wait.

"Not stubborn. Optimistic." He took in a breath and practically doubled over in pain.

"What you did for Aaron," she said quietly. "You could have injured yourself seriously, shielding him from the shards with your body the way you did. A lot of people wouldn't take that kind of risk."

Instead of answering, Sam let out a shuddering cough, then clutched his ribs and rolled over on his side.

"OK, what I'm about to do here is going to cost you *your* next piece of apple pie. Maybe two pieces, if I have on one of my transparent-in-the-rain bras." Della said as she whipped off her T-shirt to fasten around his chest as a makeshift splint. She took a quick look to see how much she was revealing, and was glad to see it was considerably less than it could have been.

"Normally I'd enjoy that," he grunted, as Della pulled the fabric around him. "But under the circumstances…"

"Well, I wouldn't be doing this if you hadn't used your shirt and jacket on Aaron," she said, opening her medical bag and pulling out a roll of cloth tape.

"If I said I need a splint on my leg, would you take off your pants?"

Della ripped a length of tape off the roll, then, as she bent over him to tape the T-shirt splint in place, she whispered in his ear, "Not a chance, Doctor. Not even for the whole pie."

"I still think you should go have an X-ray and let an emergency room doctor stitch you up," Della said, coming to a stop at the knoll. One of the firefighters had kindly offered her a jacket before she'd climbed back up the ravine and now, as her clothes were beginning to dry and stick to her skin, the cold chill of the autumn ocean breeze mixed with the leftover dampness of the rain was finally setting in. She could feel it practically all the way down to the bone. It was good to be home, such as it was, and she was looking forward to the fire working out the deep chill.

But the big question now was what would she do with Sam? He wasn't in any condition to drive, and she wasn't in any condition to take him back to his room. Maybe later, after she'd rested. For now, one thing at a time. She would tend his wounds, then afterwards figure out what to do with him.

Amazingly, for only a few hours on Redcliffe, she'd had quite a workout as a doctor. It was good to be needed. "OK, step down easily," she said as she opened the passenger door.

"I'm not an invalid," he snapped, swinging his legs out. The movement jarred him, and Sam gasped audibly.

"I don't have a proper bandage for you here," she said, as he slid out and grabbed hold of the door of the SUV for support. Della moved in under his arm to steady him and he transferred a good bit of his weight to her. Then she slung his arm around her shoulder. "Got suture for the stitches, but nothing to deaden the skin."

"Use a butterfly," he said. A taping alternative to stitches, the taping style resembled a butterfly and it was a technique of choice to use on the face or other areas of delicate skin.

"And I was looking forward to stitching in my initials." As they topped the knoll, the first thing she noticed was a light coming from the house. Then she heard the faint hum of what she assumed to be a generator. When they got closer, she saw it sitting on the front porch, along with a can of gasoline, which would keep it running throughout the night. "They're nice people," she said, as she steadied Sam up the two steps.

"Nice people who are glad to have a doctor here again."

Inside the door, Della gasped at the transformation. The house hadn't magically turned into a quaint little cottage or anything like that, but someone had brought in a cot, and not the canvas fold-up kind. It was a nice roll-away, with a mattress. There was also a wooden kitchen table with two chairs sitting next to the cot. Plus a floor lamp shining brightly in front of the plastic picture window. "I can't imagine anybody from my old life doing this," she murmured. "We were a stuffy lot, quite pretentious, awfully boring." She laughed. "Noses stuck a bit too high into the air."

"I can't see you that way," he said, pulling himself away from Della then propping himself against the doorframe. He took in several steadying breaths, then continued. "Especially with the way you look right now. The only thing sticking into the air is that stick caught in your hair."

Della reached up and plucked it out, then glanced down at herself and smiled. "Well, I suppose they wouldn't let me into the country club this way, would they?" Caked mud, torn jeans, heaven only knew what else besides twigs in her hair.

"My wife belonged to the country club. I preferred a good bicycle ride in the canyons."

"When the husband belongs, it's the wife's sworn duty to be at his side." Anthony's lecture to her on more than one occasion, and now she almost gagged on the words. "I like bicycling, too, but there wasn't enough time since I was on the ladies auxiliary board at the club." She chuckled. "Anthony was one of the club's highest financial donors, which purchased us both a position on our respective boards. He liked the glory of it, I thought it was a waste of time."

"Golf or tennis? Which was your favorite?"

"Actually, I liked the salad bar best." She laughed. "One hour before the regulars showed up so I didn't have to go on the hunt for a pretense to make small talk with them."

"My wife lived for that pretense," he said. "Golf on Mondays and Thursdays, tennis on Tuesdays and Fridays, and spa time on Wednesdays and Saturdays. Then on the seventh day she brunched with friends and rested up for the grueling week to come."

"With that kind of a schedule, I take it she wasn't a doctor."

He laughed out loud then clutched at his ribs, but didn't say a word. And from that response Della formed an impression of a woman who might have suited Anthony more than *she* had. The essential trophy wife, pretty to look at, quite acceptable in all the right social situations, and never, ever toiling twelve hours a day in a clinic for the poor. "Well, speaking of grueling, we've got to get you taken care of, and the first thing you're going to need is a bath. But I'm sure this place doesn't have running water."

"We've got running rain, though," he said, kicking off his shoes slowly. Next, he unzipped his jeans, again very gingerly, bracing himself against any undue jarring motion. "I brought some towels and washcloths with the bedding." He pointed to the heap now stacked on the cot. "Would you mind bending down to get one for me? I'm not sure my bending apparatus is quite up to it yet."

As she fetched, he began the process of sliding out of his jeans. It was such a slow, painful ordeal to watch that Della finally gave in, slung the towel and washcloth over her shoulder, then stooped to have a good tug at them. Strictly as a doctor, of course.

"Can't say I've had my doctor undress me since I was a baby," he said, still holding onto the doorframe for support. "It's not bad, though. Easily worth an extra piece of pie. Nice professional touch, Doctor," he said, chuckling.

Professional or not, it didn't feel quite so professional to Della, especially when the jeans were off and she looked up to discover she was kneeling before him while he was clad only in his boxers. That was a sight a wander-in patient didn't need to see, because apparently while she'd been busy down below he'd removed his bandage up top and the whole thing looked rather compromising right there at the front door. Quickly, Della averted her stare, fixing it on his feet as she whipped the towel and washcloth off her shoulder and handed them up to him. "Are you steady enough to do this alone?" she asked, twisting away as she stood.

"Is the doctor also offering to shower with her patient?"

Her eyes finally met his, and for a split second she thought she saw an honest question about the shower. But in a flash it was gone and the mischief was shining though. "The doctor is offering to get a bucket of water so her patient can wash off in the chair, near the fire. Alone!"

"Shower's easier," he said, grabbing the towel from her hand and making his way, very slowly, into the yard. "Don't peek," he called over his shoulder without looking back toward Della, who was trying to keep her eyes turned toward the fire now, and not the front door. "Unless you want to come scrub my back."

Once, when her eyes did wander, she saw that even in the glow from the cabin Sam was well proportioned. Muscular and tight, his body was that of an athlete and not of someone who had grown soft from sitting behind a desk, like he did now. She liked what she saw, and not in a professional way. When she became aware of the thoughts overtaking her sensibility, and the hard gaze that was now riveted to him, Della grabbed up his clothes and hurried them out to the rail on the porch, taking care *not* to look. Then she dashed back inside, rifled her bag for some fresh, gray cotton jerseys, pulled a towel off the cot and practically ran out the back door to take her own shower.

A cold shower seemed a prudent thing to do right then.

Outside, Della stripped down to her undies and tossed her dirty clothes in a pile on the covered porch, then stepped away from the house, but only far enough to allow the full force of the rain to clean her. It was chilly, causing her to shiver, but she wasn't in a hurry to go back inside. Standing there in the cold night rain, practically naked, she savored the feel of the gentle drops on her skin. It took away all the worry for a moment, made her forget the emotional torture.

As the rain beat out an even rhythm in the puddles around her, Della didn't hear the sloshing footsteps approach, neither did she see the lantern light swinging from the extended arm, until it was too late.

"Evening, ma'am," the yellow-slickered figure greeted her. "Heard you moved in. Thought I'd be neighborly and stop by to introduce myself."

Della stared at him blankly for a moment, finally let out a scream that could have been heard all the way to the mainland, then ran for the house. By the time Sam reached the front door, Della had sprinted all the way through the house and was on her way out the front of it. "There's someone in the back," she gasped, as Sam caught her by the shoulders and stopped her from running all the way out into the front yard.

Without a word, Sam made his way through the kitchen and stopped at the back door as the man opened it and stepped inside. "Evening," he said, setting a soggy box on the counter. "Odds and ends. Thought you might need a few things to get you started here." He tossed Della's dry clothes over on the opposite corner then opened the box and pulled out at least a dozen candles, seemingly unaware of the fact that Sam was standing there, practically naked. "Didn't mean to startle Doc Della, but I didn't expect to see her out back. I was going to leave the box on the porch for her to find in the morning." He pulled out an old-fashioned coffee-pot, one that would sit nicely in the fireplace, a couple of mugs and a bag of coffee. "Hope black is OK. I don't use cream and sugar in mine. And I have some tea-bags in here, if you'd rather have tea. Some bottled water, too."

For a lack of anything better to say, Sam introduced himself. "I'm Sam Montgomery," he said, wondering if extending his hand while almost in the buff was good protocol here. So he didn't. He held his spot across the room and didn't budge.

"Roger McMurtry," he said, as he pulled a couple pots from the box. "I'm from upstate New York originally, but I spend most of my time in one of the houses down the beach. Retired art teacher, current artist."

"I'm the, um…the visiting doctor. Consultant from the state commission. I'm here to oversee the start of Della's new practice."

Roger turned around to Sam and nodded without so much as a flinch over the fact that the consultant was not dressed. "Tell her I'm sorry for scaring her like I did, and that I'll come back tomorrow to have a proper introduction. There's a hole on the back porch floor, by the way, and I'll get that patched up, too, while I'm here." He smiled. "And I'll see about having the water turned on so she can shower *inside*."

With that, he plodded out the back door and let it slam shut behind him.

Sam almost felt proprietorial, which was really stupid. That artist was coming back to take care of Della tomorrow, and Sam wasn't sure he liked that. Wasn't sure he liked it that Roger had seen Della in her underwear. His proximity down the beach, a neighbor within walking distance, and one who, apparently, walked right in… No, he wasn't sure he liked that at all.

He also didn't like the fact that he didn't like it because it shouldn't have mattered. But it did.

"Just a friendly neighbor," he said as he went back to the front room and handed Della her dry clothes. She was standing by the fire, wrapped in a sheet that was open to the fire, trying to warm herself dry. He took care not to watch too hard, given his odd reaction just now. Instead, he grabbed the other sheet and wrapped it around himself, then noticed she'd retrieved his jeans from the front yard and had stretched them out to dry in front of the fireplace. Such a small thing, and so considerate. "Retired teacher, current artist, and he brought you a few supplies. That's why he was here. He'd intended to leave them on the porch for you to find in the morning."

"I'm sensing that being the doctor here comes with no expectation of privacy."

"Unless you exert yourself."

"Maybe it'll be better when I have a phone installed and they can call instead of popping in like they do." She turned to face him. "You go sit down. I'm going to take care of the stitches, then call it a night."

She looked exhausted. And that sadness he'd seen in her eyes earlier was back. "We can do it in the morning," he said.

"The doctor says no," she replied, trying to force a smile. "Just let me get dressed…" She bundled the sheet around her and padded down the hall to one of the rooms, then returned a minute later and picked up her medical bag. "Any particular design you want? Petit point, chain-stitch, French knots?"

"Doctor's choice," he said. "Would you mind giving me a hand down? From here, that cot looks awfully low." And that dash through the house had taken away nearly every last drop of strength he'd had left in him. Like Della, he wanted to go to sleep. Sleep first, then he'd try putting some sense to the strange feelings overtaking him. If there was any sense to be had.

Della braced him as he sat, then she set about her work. Her touch was surprisingly delicate as she put fifteen stitches in his arm. They did have a bit of a sting going in, and once, when he gasped, he looked up to see that she was biting her lip nervously. She relaxed a little as she prodded the wound at his hairline and closed it with her fingers, then taped it into place. He nearly shivered under her touch, she was so gentle. Then, as she wrapped a dry towel around his ribs and taped it in place, and her fingers trailed across his chest, he did shiver.

"Did I hurt you?" she asked, pulling back.

"Just a delayed reaction," he lied. It was a very immediate reaction and one he immediately put into the compartment of far too long without a woman. For the sake of his policy about not getting involved, he hoped it was true.

"Well, you're good to go."

She bent closer to have a look at her work…so close he could smell the scent of her shampoo. Peaches, he thought. She shampooed in the scent of peaches, and that was so much more than he wanted to know about her.

"Wish I had a magnifier to have a better look," she continued. "The lighting's not too good here, and I can't see it as well as I should."

She was seeing it *quite* well, in his opinion. So well, in fact, that under different circumstances this might have been considered foreplay, she was so close to him. Close, enticing… His gaze fixed on her breasts, and he was glad they weren't concealed by a lab coat. But in that same instant, when he was beginning to enjoy the nearness, he also realized what he was doing and glanced up to see if she'd caught him staring. She was still fixed on his wound but, dear God, she was moving in for an even closer look. With that, Sam gulped audibly, then shut his eyes to the temptation. Did the woman know how utterly sexy she was? he wondered.

"I think you'll be left with a rather admirable scar, considering the way you got it." She brushed back a few strands of hair that had strayed over his forehead. "Very admirable." Turning to her medical bag, she rummaged through for a bandage. "You know how to take care of this, don't you?" she asked, as she ripped off its paper. "Keep it dry—"

"How dry?" he interrupted almost frantically, his eyes still closed as he tried to force his mind off her scent, her fingers, her breasts. He cleared his throat roughly. He was a man after all. He *should* be teased by such things, but not by *her* things.

Della gave him a curious look. "Totally dry. You know that." Bending back down to Sam, she started to apply the bandage, but before she'd placed it over his wound he reached up and pulled her face to his, then brushed her lips with a light kiss. Surprisingly, in the brevity of that kiss, he wondered if she might have kissed him back. The soft press of her lips to his suggested it could have happened, but when he realized what he was doing, it came as such a shock he pulled away after he'd barely started.

"I…I don't know what to say," he said quickly, amazed that she wasn't reacting. "I'm sorry. I don't normally do things like that." Instead of slapping him or kicking him out of her house, she was still coming at him with the bandage. And here he was going almost woozy over something as slight as a kiss. Although, as kisses went, it had been a good one.

"There's nothing to say if that's the way you are with all your doctors," she replied, her voice composed as she finally pressed the bandage to his skin. "But if it's not the way you are with your other doctors, keep in mind that I'm the one who's about to give you a tetanus shot, and my needle technique has a direct bearing on my mood. I'm in a good mood if that was merely an expression of your appreciation for my medical work. I'm not in a good mood if that was an expression of anything else."

She was good. Sassy, smart. Fast with a retort. If it hadn't been for the fact that Della's next go at him would be with a needle in her hand, he'd kiss her again. "Definitely my appreciation for your work," he replied, giving her a rueful smile. "The way I kiss all my doctors, except Doc Reilly, and he prefers a more circumspect handshake."

Della pulled an extraordinarily large syringe from her medical bag, waved it at him, smiled and arched her eyebrows wickedly. "I thought so." Then she tucked it away and pulled out a needle that looked much more reasonable. "Now, where would you like it?"

Her technique at giving a shot was swift and relatively painless, and by the time the bleeding from the tiny pinprick had stopped, he was tired, almost to the point of exhaustion, with a little residual embarrassment still lingering, and definitely ready for some sleep. It had been a long, hard day topped off with unexpected feelings he didn't fully understand and was tempted to attribute to side-effects of his head injury. All he wanted to do now was put his aching head down on a soft pillow, close his eyes, and figure it all out in the morning. "If you could help me to my car now, I'll come back tomorrow with that whole pie I owe you since you *did* take off your pants."

She smiled. "Just half a pie, since I removed my pants for personal reasons." Then she pointed to the cot. "And that's as far as you're going tonight. You can't drive, and I don't want to. If you can keep your lips to yourself, you're invited to stay."

"Are you sure?" he asked, even though he knew he shouldn't do it. One kiss and he wanted more.

"I broke your ribs. It's the least I can do." She pulled one of the blankets off the bedding pile, doubled it and spread it on the floor. Then she turned off the floor lamp, pulled off another blanket and wrapped it around herself like a cocoon, grabbed a pillow and sat down. "And in the morning, if you're the first one up, you make the coffee."

She lay down, and within seconds he heard the gentle breathing of sleep coming from her. Helping her like he'd done, sleeping here with her like he was about to do…this definitely wasn't in his job description. Not even close to it. But he'd deal with that later. Get back on track, try to regain his wandering perspective, reboot his objectivity. All that in the morning, right after he made her coffee.

As he shut his eyes, Sam thought about the kiss again. He could still feel it on his lips. Sighing, he smiled. She *had* kissed him back.

CHAPTER SIX

MORNING dawned bright and, blessedly, without rain. Della opened her eyes slowly, listening to the call of the gulls outside and thinking about the kiss. It had been nothing, really. She and Sam had both been tired. Exhausted. They'd shared an intense situation in the rescue and the kiss had been part of the emotional aftermath. It had merely been one of those moments. It had happened, it was over. That's all! She would simply put it out of her mind and act adult about it. She really did like Sam after all, and she wasn't about to let something as impetuous as a little kiss end the friendship before it had barely begun. So, it was out of her mind. No more. It was as if nothing had happened between them.

Still, as Della squinted her eyes in the sunlight filtering in through the plastic window coverings, she brushed her fingers lightly over her lips, then turned over to have a look at Sam. She was greeted by eyes looking down at her that weren't his.

"You said to come back in the morning," Gina Showalter said, her face so grim Della wanted to pull the blanket up over her head and start today much later on.

"Have you been here long?" she asked, sitting up, pushing the hair back from her eyes. She took a quick glance around for

Sam, but didn't see him anywhere. Didn't see his jeans drying at the fireplace, didn't see his shoes at the foot of the cot.

"A little while. I stayed outside first, then came in when the other doctor left. He told me to help myself to some coffee." She was clutching a mug, and Della saw that the coffee in it was barely touched. She also saw that Sam had placed the home pregnancy test on the floor under the cot.

"Have you ever taken one of these before?" Della asked, picking up the box.

Gina shook her head. "When we…you know, it was the first time I ever did that. And I really didn't think I could get pregnant on the first time. And we didn't mean to, well, you know…do the whole thing."

Famous last words before motherhood, Della thought. "I guess we'll know in about five minutes if that's what happened." She explained the test to Gina, then sent her into the bathroom. While she was in there, Della got up, dashed out to the porch to have a look over the knoll. Sam's SUV wasn't there. Just as well, she thought. Getting so dependent on someone so quickly wasn't a good thing. Already she'd become used to having him around, and that's not what this part of her life was about. Later, she would go to the village to call Meghan and get her utilities turned on, and maybe she'd run into him. Of course, maybe she wouldn't. It shouldn't matter one way or the other, but as she walked back into the house and saw the cot where he'd spent the night, she realized that it did matter just the slightest.

"So, now what do I do?" Gina called from the bathroom.

"Wait," Della called back as she poured herself a cup of the coffee Sam had made. Instead of sitting back down to enjoy it, though, she wandered down the hall and leaned on the wall outside the bathroom to await the verdict. "So, do you want a baby, Gina?" she called.

"No. Not until…" She paused. "Not until I'm older."

Her voice sounded on the verge of tears, and Della's heart went out to her. She'd been twenty-five when she'd discovered she was pregnant, and even then it had been a shock because she and Anthony had never settled on the parenting issue. She couldn't begin to image what Gina felt like right now, going through this so young and alone.

Soon, Gina poked the test strip out the door. "Can't look at it," she said.

Della did, though. "Not pregnant," she said, relieved for the girl.

"Are you sure?"

"Check it yourself, Gina. If you're going to indulge in this sort of activity without protecting yourself, you'll have to learn to read it." That sounded a bit harsh perhaps, but Gina was old enough to take responsibility, because the result of irresponsibility could bring about a whole set of new responsibilities. Judging from how nervous Gina was about all this, those were responsibilities she didn't want yet.

Gina pulled the test strip back in, shut the bathroom door, then ten seconds later opened it, smiling sheepishly. "Is it accurate?" she asked.

"Normally, yes. But if you don't get your period in another week, I'm going to have to do an examination. And in the meantime, Gina, use protection. It's not only a pregnancy issue these days."

"I know, but he said he's too embarrassed to go to the pharmacy."

"Then go to the mainland. You're putting so much at risk if you don't." There was always such a balance treating teenagers—too little and the message didn't sink in, too much and it was ignored. Half her patients at the clinic had been young and getting through to them had been a solemn responsibility; one she hadn't taken lightly. "You can pick up some-

thing that will change your life, recur over and over, prevent
you from having children, affect your overall health. And it's
not worth it. Trust me, I've seen lives ruined because someone
didn't want to use the proper protection." She paused and took
a sip of coffee. "So, do you plan on college?"

Gina nodded. "MIT." Massachusetts Institute of Technology.
"I'm going to be a mechanical engineer."

"How exciting!" She had such a bright future, and Della
prayed she wouldn't waste her opportunities.

"I have a scholarship."

"A scholarship to MIT's quite an accomplishment! Congratulations, Gina." Della thought about the rest of the lecture,
starting with, *Don't mess up your future.* But she didn't go any
further. Sometimes actions spoke louder than words, and the
near repercussions of Gina's actions had certainly scared her.
If she wanted her future, she would be careful. "Just take care
of yourself, OK?" she said instead. "And after I'm set up, I'd
still like to do a complete physical."

So maybe something she'd said would sink in. She hoped
so, anyway, for Gina's sake.

After she had gone, Della washed her face in a bucket of water
she found on the kitchen cabinet, then dragged a comb through
her hair. Heading outside, she paused for a moment, looking out
over the beach. It was breathtaking. A perfect place for Meghan.
She could picture them playing together in the sand, looking for
seashells, going wading. It had been a little over twenty-four
hours since she'd heard her daughter's voice, and that was the
first item on her agenda, right after finding her clinic.

It was actually a pleasant walk down the path. The Atlantic
Ocean was on her right, different kinds of vegetation, which
she vowed to learn the names of, to her left, and once she
rounded the barn she spotted a small building. It sat back in

a little grove of grasses, many of which were half as tall as the building. From a distance it looked as though the ravages of time hadn't been so harsh as elsewhere. And what a charming place to have a clinic.

The clapboard of the small structure was weathered but not rotting. Perhaps a nice coat of paint was all an outside facelift would take. The clinic was actually set off from its landscape by a white picket fence at the front, which, like the clapboard, needed some fresh paint, too. For no good reason, Della felt her hopes starting to rise the closer she got. If the inside was no worse than the outside, this would be a marvelous clinic, and quite possibly she might have it in shape to operate within a few days.

When she stepped inside, though, her hopes dropped. There was nothing there. Absolutely nothing. The structure was sound, and overall in decent shape, but there wasn't one speck of the medical equipment she'd been expecting. Not an examining room, not a waiting area, not even a peg on which to hang a coat. It was simply one long, rectangular room, with a tiny, boxed-off bathroom in the far corner and a single cabinet with a sink under the window overlooking the beach.

"So how did they make it work?" she asked, walking to the far end to look out the window. In the distance she saw several other such structures, all practically identical to this one. The artists' colony, she supposed. She could see why artists would want to come there to paint, it was so beautiful. And so isolated. It gave her a little shiver, thinking how utterly alone she was out here.

"It all depends on what you want, I suppose," she said as she shut the door on the way out. "If it's beauty and isolation, this is the place." She chuckled. "It would have driven you insane, Anthony," she said to no one but the gull staring up at her from a rock on the beach. "Maybe it would have kept you faithful to our marriage, too."

More water under the bridge. And there was so much of it, sometimes it seemed like the floodgates had opened full force on her. "But I can swim," she said resolutely, as she headed for the barn. In size, it wasn't a typical country barn, but more of a miniature version. Like the clinic and all the artists' quarters, it was painted white, and once she stepped inside she saw, well, nothing. At the very least she'd hoped for the medical equipment she'd been promised as part of the deal, but all she found were a couple of empty horse stalls, a small tractor and various yard tools.

The idea of a horse or pony for Meghan popped into her mind. "When you're a little older," she said, as if Meghan was there, arguing to get her pony.

Sighing, Della left the barn then walked out to the beach. Impulsively, she kicked off her shoes and wiggled her toes into the sand. It was smooth and still warm, but not hot against her skin as she might find it in the heat of summer. "We own a beach, Meghan," she whispered, as she rolled up her pink gauzy pants and waded into the water. "Can you believe it, sweetie? We own our very own beach." Her toe caught on a sharp object…a shell, she discovered as she fished it out of the water. Just like she didn't know her plants, she didn't know her shells, but this was pearly white on the outside and a shiny pink on the inside. It snuggled perfectly into the palm of her hand, and she held onto it for a moment, examining its every facet before she stuck it into her pocket. Later today she would find a small box and send it to Meghan.

This could be a good life, she decided. If she could figure out where her medical equipment was.

The village was quiet when she pulled in. In the distance, the merry toot of Captain Cecil's ferry horn announced that the back-and-forth shuttle was preparing to leave for the mainland. At the end of the block, she saw all the people hustling on board, some by auto, some by foot, and it surprised her how many of them actually commuted. Of course, resources were quite limited here. Self-sufficiency was the lifestyle, but it did need help.

Later, if she had time, she would take a hop across the water to the hospital, not only to look in on the three boys she'd sent over last night, but also to meet the people there who would be her second line of help. Maybe she'd also hook into their medical suppliers and set up a line of supply for herself. First, though, Meghan.

Della pulled her car into a spot on the street across from the grocery and headed to the public phone near the corner. It was tucked back into a quaint patch of quince bushes, down a short brick pathway. Everything here was so well kept, she thought as she fished through her purse for her phone card. The Riordans had told her to call collect, quite condescendingly, but she wasn't about to be beholden to them for anything, even the shortest of phone calls, so once her card was in hand she punched in all the right numbers, then waited for someone to answer the phone at the other end.

After three rings she heard the voice that she'd come, lately, to despise. "She's eating her breakfast," Vivian said. "Would you call back later?"

"No," Della said, trying not to snap. "I don't have a phone installed yet, and I'm not sure when I can get back to the village. It might be past her bedtime."

"Which is why she was taken away from you," Vivian retorted. "You don't know how to follow traditional rules when it comes to caring for children. You don't set schedules."

Schedules. Traditional rules. Being the best mother she could possibly be, caring for her child, living with her child…that sounded traditional to her. But the Riordan definition of tradition came in the objects they possessed and the clout they exerted. Della quite literally bit her lip to keep from saying all the things that wanted to pop right out, most of them having to do with Vivian's son. But she didn't, for if she did, anything she said would be used to keep her from Meghan. And nothing was stipulated in court about allowing her phone calls, meaning the Riordans could cut them off altogether if they wanted. So she bit her lip and drew in a deep breath. "I don't want to disrupt her schedule," she said, trying to sound even about it.

"Which you are already doing." Vivian expelled a loud, exaggerated sigh over the phone. "But I suppose if you have to… We have a morning routine. She looks forward to our walks together."

Della knew that walk. She'd watched it every morning since Meghan had been taken away. It was down a stone promenade lined with other houses. Meghan would love a walk on the beach so much better. "I'm sure she does," Della said.

"So, please, be brief about it."

Please, be brief about it. Those words tore through Della's heart like a dull scalpel, and she fought hard against the tears that were already stinging her eyes because she didn't want Meghan to hear the sadness in her voice. Instead, she pulled the tiny picture frame out of her pocket and concentrated on the photo of her daughter until Meghan finally exploded onto the line.

"Mommy," she squealed, sounding delighted. "Grandma got me a new puppy. He's got long ears and big eyes and I named him Scooter because his belly scoots along the floor."

A puppy? Anthony had never allowed pets. "I can't wait to meet him, sweetie. Maybe you can draw a picture of him and send it to me."

"He's little now, but Grandma says he'll get bigger, and

maybe even his ears will drag on the ground, too. He's some kind of a hound, I think."

"A basset hound?"

"I think so. And we take him on walks with us."

"Maybe you could draw me a picture of you taking him on a walk."

"If Grandma lets me. She said you went away because you didn't have time to take care of me. Will you have time to look at my picture?"

Della squeezed her eyes shut. "I do have time for you, sweetie. I always have, and you know that. You're the most important person in my life. But right now I'm trying to get things ready so we'll have a brand-new place to live, and I don't even have any water or lights yet." She wanted to tell her of the beautiful beach and the seashell and how she would buy her a pony, but in the background Vivian was telling Meghan to hang up. And Della hadn't heard nearly enough of her daughter's voice yet.

"When can I go to the new house, Mommy?"

"In a little while, sweetie. In a little while." The sting of tears was overcoming her now and she could hear the quiver in her voice. "I'll call you as often as I can and tell you everything I'm doing to get our new house ready."

"Will you draw me a picture?"

"I sure will, sweetie. I sure will."

"Grandma says we have to stay on the schedule, so I've got to go, Mommy."

"I'll call you again, sweetie, just as soon as I can."

"Byebye, Mommy."

"I love you, Meghan. Remember that. I love you so much."

She wasn't sure Meghan even heard the last words, but it didn't matter. In the future, when they were together, she would hear it every day, several times a day. Della swiped the back of her hand across her eyes to brush away the tears, then stepped out onto the sidewalk, directly into Sam.

"Bad news?" he asked, giving her a puzzled look.

Had he been listening? Standing behind the bushes, listening to her conversation with Meghan? It occurred to her that he might have, but Sam didn't seem the type to listen in on a private chat. "No," she replied, trying to sound indifferent. "Nothing bad. Just taking care of matters back home."

"And let me guess, you're already homesick."

"Not homesick," she said, then changed the subject. "Are you feeling better?"

"Feeling like I spent the night on a lumpy cot, favoring a few broken ribs. And you?"

"Had my first patient already this morning. Oh, and I had a nice cup of coffee, too. Thanks for doing that."

"It's not so bad doing it when waiting hand and foot on m'lady isn't second on my list of chores." He smiled. "And it was. Sometimes my ex-wife moved it to the top."

"What was first on the list when you weren't waiting on her hand and foot?"

"Making a fortune. Third was diamonds, rubies, emeralds, cars, furs. Lots and lots of them."

Della laughed. Somehow, she couldn't picture Sam in that lifestyle. She couldn't even picture him anywhere near it. "She must have lived in high style."

"Not high enough, especially when she found out the diamonds were really zircons and the furs *faux*. I called the hospital this morning, by the way. Aaron and Marty are on the mend, but it's still touch and go for Bart. The surgery was successful—they removed his spleen and got the bleeding stopped—but he's still on the critical list, and they're watching him for infection because they found a small perforation in his bowel."

"All for a little thrill ride in the mud. Hardly seems worth it. But you don't think about those things at the time, do you?" Much like the way she hadn't thought about so many things when she'd married Anthony. "Anyway, I was thinking about going over to see them later, if I have time. After I attend to my own list."

"Me waiting on you hand and foot isn't on it, by any chance, is it?"

She smiled halfheartedly. "No, but I could add it."

"Been there. Don't want to do that again. So, do you need some help? Got pretty much nothing to do for the rest of the day."

"Right now I'm on my way to have my utilities turned on, then set up an appointment to have a phone installed. After that some grocery shopping, then picking up some books at the library. It's all single-person stuff, but I appreciate the offer." His company would have been nice, even if he'd done nothing more than tag along. Which was why she was refusing him. Talking with Meghan had reminded her of how on focus she needed to keep herself, and Sam Montgomery could be the distraction to ruin all that if she let him. Which she wouldn't. "So the doctor says it's a good day for some bed rest. Give those ribs some time to heal."

"Broken ribs heal with, or without, bed rest, and as broken ribs go, mine aren't so tender this morning. And in case you're interested, your utilities are being turned on today. I saw to that a little while ago. The phone will be put in sometime tomorrow, too. As for the groceries, I have several bagsful in the back of my SUV, thanks to a very kind lady named…" He frowned. "Can't remember it, but she was nice and she flagged me down a few minutes ago and asked me to take them out to you. Also, Sharon, the librarian, stopped me with an armload of books you requested. So it looks like I've done all your errands."

Della drew in a deep breath to steady herself. She knew Sam was trying to be helpful, but she simply didn't need his help. It would be too easy to become dependent on it…on him. All she'd asked for yesterday had been directions to her house. That, and nothing else. For that simple request she'd gotten herself into an involvement she didn't want. "Look, Sam, let me be honest with you. I like you, and I appreciate the fact that you're trying to help me, but when I told you yesterday that I'm not up for a relationship, I meant it. I'm not…not interested in any sort of personal involvement. My life is a mess in ways you couldn't even begin to understand, and I've got things to do in order to straighten it out. I can't do that if I'm being distracted."

"So what you're saying here is that I distract you?"

He gave her an innocently sexy grin—one that would have melted her resolve if she'd let it. But she wouldn't, and she averted her eyes to be safe from the kind of distraction that shocked her…the physical kind, the kind that looked at Sam in a way other than someone to lean on. It had been a good long while since she'd had that reaction to anyone. Certainly those feelings for Anthony had died long before he had.

Now the little tingle running all the way through her…had she ever had it for her husband? Or for anyone? Too long without a man, she decided. That's all it was, all it could be. Too long without physical affection. This was her body's reaction…her hormones, her libido. As a physician, she could understand that. But as a woman? "You distract me in more ways than you know," she whispered. "In so many more ways than you know. And I can't allow that to happen, because I have another priority which is so much more important than anything else."

"I suppose you're not going to tell me what that is?"

Della shook her head. "No," she said, purposely stepping

back from him. Right now, even the proximity was distracting her. "I'm not. And I'm sorry to be so blunt about this, but depending on you like I've been doing isn't putting my life together. I know you've got some kind of official duty overseeing my progress here, and I'll respect that and co-operate with whatever it is you need from me. But on a personal level we've just got to let it go, Sam. This is *my* life and I've got to learn to get along in it. You'll be gone in another couple of weeks anyway."

"Point taken, Doctor," he said rather stiffly.

"I'm sorry, Sam."

"So am I, Della. For more reasons than you know, so am I."

It had been five days now, and she hadn't seen Sam once in that time. Someone had told her he'd left the island, but Mrs Hawkins said he still had the room reserved at her bed and breakfast for another week. She confirmed for Della, though, that he hasn't used it lately.

Today, as Della alternately took *before* photos to show the judge her progress, stripped away the old wallpaper from the front room of her house and took *after* photos to chart her efforts, she couldn't get Sam off her mind. Up until now she'd been busy day and night, seeing a steady stream of patients in and out her door, as well as working on all the home improvement chores she'd discovered were necessary after reading all the do-it-yourself books Sharon had sent around. Little things—putting rubber washers in her old faucets and cleaning out the roof gutters. Big things—patching wall boards and re-nailing floorboards. Her plan was to make the place minimally habitable then move on to the clinic and put it into perfect repair.

"Are you sure I can't do something?" Stuart Jennings called from the kitchen, where he was stretched out on a cot.

He was having a diabetic reaction, and instead of having him
trek to her house four times a day for a check, or her having
to trek to the far end of the island to his isolated little patch
of land, she'd set up a makeshift hospital bed in her kitchen.
That way she could stay at home and accomplish more work,
while looking after him at the same time. The house was
clean now, still shabby but at least a fit place for patient care,
and Stuart didn't care in the least that he was bedded straight
across from the refrigerator. He said he rather liked the hum
of it, that it was soothing.

"Until I get your blood sugar leveled out, I don't want you
up and about. That's what got you here in the first place, wandering around with your blood sugar so low you passed out
and hit your head." Stuart was a nice man, probably somewhere near seventy, and it was driving him absolutely crazy,
being there. He had a potter's shed at home, and now that he
was retired from banking on the mainland he made beautiful
pots. She looked at the fireplace mantle, at a lovely piece he'd
fashioned for her in payment for his first office call—the one
where she'd discovered him standing barefoot at her front
door, pot in hand, with a rather large gash on his cheek.

Della smiled as she looked up at his vase. On the open
market, a Stuart Jennings piece brought a handsome price.
She'd had one when she'd been with Anthony. Sold at the tax
auction, of course. But now she had another—one with all the
colors of her beach—and she cherished it. "One more day and
if you're still holding up well, you can go home." She heard
him turn on the small television the Landerses had brought
over in partial payment for her treatment of their sons. Stuart
had been complaining for the past twenty-four hours over her
lack of a satellite dish for better reception and more channels,
but in spite of complaining, he made do with the few channels
he could get.

Amazing, she thought as she grabbed hold of a strip of paper and peeled it off the wall. She had *the* Stuart Jennings sleeping on a cot in her kitchen. Even Vivian Riordan couldn't help but be impressed over that.

Della was so intent on trying to get one long strip of paper pulled away, instead of ripping it into several small, impossible scraps, that she didn't hear her screen door open. It was only when it slammed shut that she looked up. "Sam" she said, blinking in surprise.

"It's coming along," he said. "Looks like you have only a layer or two more to pull off."

"It's one wall. I've spent five *long* days working on one wall." Progress, yes. But dreadfully slow. And irritating. More than that, she was irritated with Sam over his disappearance then sudden reappearance. No, he didn't owe her an explanation, especially after the way she'd put him off. But she was irritated all the same. That she was bothered by that irritated her even more.

"I wanted to help her, but she's stubborn and wouldn't even let me out of bed," Stuart shouted from the kitchen.

Sam was the one to blink in surprise this time, and he gave Della a puzzled look.

"He's a patient," she explained hastily. "Keeps going hypoglycemic. Passed out, had a nasty fall, so he's staying here now so I can look after him, monitor his blood sugar on a regular basis, make sure he's eating properly."

"You turned your kitchen into a hospital?" he asked, his voice edging on stiffness.

"More like an observation area. Stuart lives alone. Somebody had to look after him."

"I came for an exam and she's holding me hostage," he called out. "Doesn't even have a satellite dish for the television."

"You better behave, Stuart," Della warned, "or next time

I'll move Mrs Fontana's cot in right next to yours. And you know how she loves to talk."

"Mrs Fontana?" Sam asked.

"Case of indigestion. She stayed one night, more for support than actual medical treatment. Although I'm going to have her tested for an ulcer next week. She's a little bit tender to prodding, and she's having too many episodes of gastric upset."

"Since I've been gone you've had two patients stay here." This time his voice was definitely stiff. No mistaking it.

Della let her strip of paper drop loose from her hands and walked over to him. "Is that a problem?" she whispered, so Stuart wouldn't overhear.

"You don't meet the standards to call this a hospital, Della. It's a…a hovel. It won't pass as a clinic, and it certainly won't pass as a hospital."

"So the next time a patient comes here on the verge of hypoglycemic shock, I'm supposed to do what? Tell him to find his way to the dock and hope Captain Cecil can take him over to Connaught before he passes out and possibly dies? And what if the patient refuses other treatment, such as Stuart did? What do I do with him then?" She had started at a quiet level and by the time her last words were out her voice was practically shrill.

"Hell, no, I won't go," Stuart chimed in from the kitchen.

"You convince him," Sam said. "Call a medical transport to take him out of here."

"Against his will? Some people would call that kidnaping." She huffed out an exasperated breath and swiped the hair back from her face. "Look, Sam, under the circumstances, I'm doing the best I can here. I've got a steady stream of patients coming in, and no one's complaining about the conditions. I figure if they can put up with them temporarily, I can certainly give them the treatment they need. They all know my situation, and everybody's being very good about it."

"I'm not!" This from Stuart.

"Is it time for me to draw another blood sample?" she called back, fighting against a smile.

Stuart didn't answer this time. Didn't say a word.

"He's a nice man," she explained. "Rather a curmudgeon, but nice."

"He's a curmudgeon who can't stay in your kitchen, Della. Don't you understand that? He can't stay."

"I understand that I can't run this place as a hospital, and I'm not doing that. Not in any sense. And if you had a look around, you'd see that."

"I'd see a patient under care on a bed in your kitchen. That's what I'd see, Della."

"Why are you being so unreasonable about this, Sam? You know I didn't have another choice here, so is this attitude because I didn't want to get involved with you? Are you being so bullheaded because I told you I didn't have room in my life for an involvement?" She could understand hurt feelings, especially if he'd been developing feelings for her. But he'd come back here so stubborn and stiff, and that didn't seem at all like him. "Because, if that's the case, I'm not backing down from what I told you about personal relationships, and I'm not treating my patients any differently than I've been doing. It all works for me, Sam, and in my life, that's all that counts."

"Lovers' quarrel?" Stuart piped up.

Both Sam and Della looked at the kitchen door, then they slowly looked back at each other. "I still want to be friends, Sam, if you can do that on my terms." She smiled, trying to ease the tension between them, and her voice softened. "It was nice having another doctor around, and when you're here I would like to consider you a friend as well as a professional colleague, if we can manage that."

"And that's all you want, Della? Just another doctor here?"

His voice was still stiff and his face set in a rigid frown. Maybe he didn't want to be her friend. Maybe she'd already pushed him too far away. "It's all I can have, Sam. Right now, it's all I can have, and if you're looking for something else, just get out! I don't want it, and I don't want you."

They both waited for a response from Stuart, but when none came Sam continued, "I can be your friend, Della, but as a friend I'm concerned by the way you're operating your medical practice. What you're doing isn't up to standard. And, yes, I know you're in a bad position, but that doesn't change the fact that this overall situation is not a good one. You shouldn't be treating patients under these conditions and even allowing them to stay here. Can you accept that I'm worried over that?"

Della nodded, but didn't respond. Even though he'd said the words, his voice was still stiff. Maybe not quite so much as before, but it wasn't the warm tone she'd already come to expect from him.

"The hell of it is," Stuart finally piped up, "men like you always want more from women like her. First you're concerned about her medical practices, then you're concerned about her *other* practices. After that, the only thing you're concerned about is doing a little private practice on her!"

Sam stared wide-eyed at Della, suddenly fighting back the laugh tugging at him. "Is he like that all the time?" he whispered.

"Actually, he's behaving well right now."

Sam's face sobered a bit. "If that's his good behavior…" Giving his head a skeptical shake, Sam pulled Della out of earshot of the kitchen. "All I'm trying to say here, Della, is don't push me away and read ulterior motives into everything I'm doing. OK? I'm trying to be your friend, and whatever it was that burned you in the past has nothing to do with me. So, can we start over?"

"What burned me was my husband," she said, with absolutely no emotion in her voice. "He cheated on me and left me destitute when he died. He had habits, Sam. Bad habits with his money, and I never saw it. Or if I did, I pushed them aside and pretended I didn't know because I didn't want to know."

"You don't have to tell me," he said softly, reaching out to rub his thumb along her cheek.

"If we're to be friends, I do." She smiled up at him, glad to have him back. She wasn't sure for how long, or how it would work out. But deep down, in a way she shouldn't, she trusted Sam as she had never trusted another person in her life. It was, indeed, good to have him back in her life, even if the terms of it were uncertain.

"Now it's time for the make-up kiss," Stuart called. "Don't let me stop you."

Della thought about it for a second, thought she might allow it. But at that exact moment Sam walked over to the wall and grabbed hold of the strip of paper she'd been tearing off and began to pull.

"Don't hear anything yet," Stuart shouted. "Not a damned thing."

Trouble was, she did hear something. It was the beat of her heart, and the rhythm was almost as mixed up as she was.

CHAPTER SEVEN

DELLA'S hands trembled as she looked at the pictures Meghan had drawn. Meghan and Scooter in several poses—playing in the yard, going for a walk. The pictures had arrived in the morning mail and the black crayon words scrawled at the bottom of the one she held in her hand had been made with some effort. Meghan had known how to print for well over a year now, but some of the letters still confused her, and the "n" in Meghan was backwards. Della swiped away a tear. That one was always tricky for her.

She thought about putting the picture on the refrigerator, but with so much in and out commotion in her house all the time she was afraid it would be damaged, so she tucked it back into its envelope, vowing to frame it when she had the time, and for now take it out for a look whenever she was feeling blue. Which was right now. She was very blue. Her last two phone calls to her daughter had been refused. Meghan hadn't been available to come to the phone, according to Vivian. Furthermore, there was no certainty that she would be available at the next phone call. That, according to Vivian again.

Today there were no patients in the kitchen, and so far no one had stopped by for an appointment. She hadn't even seen Sam since the day they'd negotiated a truce of sorts on their relationship. Two days ago, to be exact. He'd stayed on to help strip wallpaper for about an hour, then he had gone. Once, after that, she'd seen him on the street in Redcliffe, coming off the ferry, and he'd waved, but he'd made no attempt to stop her for a chat.

"It's what you wanted," she said, her voice so glum it blended into the heaps of peeled wallpaper. "You set the rules, he followed them. So get over it." Della forced herself up off the cot, tucked the letter from Meghan under the pillow, and walked to the front door. She'd been on the island over a week now, and the progress was so slow. She needed a home, but more than that she needed a medical clinic. There would come a point when the novelty of having a doctor on the island would wear off and the people would become less tolerant of the conditions under which they were examined. "I need a plan," she said, stepping outside and looking at the beach.

There was a chill in the air today, and she gathered her sweater around her and headed down to the sand. "A real plan. Not just a make-do way to pass the day." Which was what she'd been doing. She was over four weeks into the six months granted by the judge, and so far her momentum was all forward, but not fast enough in her estimation. "Not nearly fast enough," she said, stopping halfway between her house and the water. "I'm just going sideways." Going from project to project, working hard, and not accomplishing nearly what she demanded of herself.

"Crabs do it all the time," Sam said, walking up behind her.

She hadn't heard him approach, and she gasped when he spoke. "And crabs end up being eaten," she said, purposely not turning to look at him. "Put them into a pot with vegetables and you've got a nice crab boil. Maybe the crab might have gotten away if he'd only moved forward. Or maybe he got what he deserved because he didn't. Either way, it doesn't matter when he ends up on the supper plate, does it?"

"Sounds like you're not having a very good day," he said, his voice thick with sympathy. He moved up behind Della and slid his arm around her waist.

She didn't resist. It had been so long since she'd been touched, and this felt good. "We're all entitled," she said on a sigh.

"Am I hearing twinges of giving in?"

"I can see why the others before me did. It's not easy here, Sam. I work hard all day, and at the end of the day when I step back to take a look at my accomplishments, I can't see anything. It all looks the same as it did when I started. And I'm running out of time."

"Running out of time?"

She hadn't meant to say that. "Before winter," she lied. "I wanted to have everything in good order by winter, but time's running out." She liked the feel of him pressed to her, even if it was merely a gesture of friendship. Anthony had never been kind that way. His physical advances had been sexual, never supportive. If he'd slipped his arm around her waist, the next move had been to the bedroom. But Sam's touch felt so different, so good. So right. She leaned her head lightly against his shoulder, shut her eyes and listened to the sound of the gulls swarming off the shoreline looking for their first meal of the day. This moment was a perfect place in time. Sadly, it would last for only a moment. "I suppose I should get to work," she finally said, pulling away from him yet still not looking at him.

"How about taking a few hours off and having some fun?"

Fun was a term very foreign to her vocabulary these days. She was tempted. More than that, she was distracted. But that wasn't good. She had to stay focused, there was no debating that fact. "I wish I could, but I can't. I've got another wall to strip, then I have to go to Connaught this afternoon to meet with a medical supplier. He has a line on some used office equipment for me."

"So do I," Sam said. "Hell of a deal, too good to refuse."

That caused her to finally turn around. "Last time someone said that, this is what I got." She gestured wide to indicate the expanse of her property.

He smiled. "But it remains to be seen if that's bad or good, and with some equipment to fill your office, that tilts it more toward the good than it was, I should think."

"Always a fool for a handsome face," she murmured.

"Is that in reference to me?"

"You, among others. So, tell me about this equipment."

"It's been in storage, waiting for a new home. And it's free, if you want it. Although there's a shipping cost involved. I didn't want to give the go-ahead to have it shipped…no stepping on toes." He kicked a little sand over the toe of her shoe. "It's your decision. If you want it, give me the word and it will be sent out in a few days. If you don't…"

"If I don't!" she practically squealed. "Of course I want it. But what's the catch?"

"No catch. I simply ran into someone who no longer had a use for it, and he was glad to send it to a good home."

She was stunned, almost to the point of being speechless. "I…I don't know what to say. This was turning into such an awful day, then suddenly…" She smiled, almost demurely. "I'm not used to having things like this happening to me. For the longest time my luck has been so bad, sometimes to the point that I wondered if it was even worth getting out of bed to see what the next bad patch coming my way was. So, can I call him? Say thank you, maybe promise him an original Stuart Jennings, since I have quite a few of them now?"

"I think he prefers it to remain an anonymous gesture."

"Then, please, tell him for me that if he ever needs a guest cottage on a beach, I'll have one ready for him." She reached out and squeezed Sam's hand. "And, Sam, thank you for arranging this. Especially since I haven't been the nicest with you."

"Is there a guest cottage on the beach in this for me someday, too?"

"Any time you want it. But you might want to wait until it's a bit more fixed up."

"There's one more thing I really want, though," he said, smiling.

"I'm almost afraid to ask."

"Dinner in Connaught tonight. Nothing fancy. I know a nice little seafood restaurant on the pier. We'll go over, spend a couple of hours there, and come home. Simply between friends." He crossed his heart to promise.

"Between friends," she repeated as she nodded her acceptance. "And in the meantime, I've got to figure out what to do with my medical equipment when it arrives. Do you know how much of it there is?"

"Two complete exam rooms, some of the admin pieces, like a desk and file cabinet."

She frowned. That was much more than the small white guest cottage could accommodate. Of course, another option was to rent a place in town. But that would leave her in the same pickle as before—taking Meghan along to the office. The judge had forbidden it once and most likely he would again. So it was back to the drawing board with the cottage. On a good note, it wasn't nearly as rundown as her house. That was the second bit of optimism for the day.

"So, what's that about?" he asked, pointing to her frown.

"Trying to figure out how I'm going to set up office." She smiled. "It was easier when I didn't have actual medical equipment to contend with."

"Can't help you with that one. My wife always accused me

of total ineptitude when it came to any sort of skill in design. She did it all herself. The house, my office."

"Anthony hired someone. He said my tastes ran to early shanty, and I guess he was right." Laughing, she smiled up at him. "Just look at me now!"

"Ah, but a shanty is in the eye of the beholder."

"And quite possibly in the eye of the board of medical standards who will undoubtedly send some stodgy old inspector out one of these days to have a look at what I'm doing here."

Sam raised his eyebrows over that, but didn't comment.

A few patients had trickled in over the course of the day. Sam had returned to the village, then gone over to Connaught on business, while Della had taken care of a sprained elbow, a rash, a seasonal allergy, a headache, and a couple of other things. The day actually went by quite quickly, and in between patients she was putting her new plan to paper. Getting the previous clinic back up to standard was the main thing. New floors, redo the walls, build some partitions for privacy, new plumbing… It could work, and she'd even asked John Hesper, her patient with a sprained elbow, if he thought it was a feasible plan. Since he was a builder, she'd figured he would know. He'd promised to return in a few days to have a good look around and give her a preliminary estimate on the cost of the major work involved. That was exciting.

Of course, knowing that the conversion was possible and actually engaging in it were two separate things. "One step at a time," she whispered, as she waited on the dock for Captain Cecil's ferry. Even with an estimate, there wasn't an assurance she could manage all the work right away. But certainly she could have a go at it by herself in the beginning. And take photos to show the judge. An honest record of what she was trying to accomplish should count for something. She hoped so, anyway.

Suddenly, Della felt excited—it was the first real excitement she'd felt in months. The old optimism was returning, and while she thought an evening with Sam would be pleasant, she was already wishing she could get back home and have a go at the clinic—take another walk-through, sketch designs, take measurements. It seemed such a waste to lose these hours. But after all a promise was a promise, and as much as she needed to back out on dinner with Sam, she wouldn't. Another time would have been better, though—a time when all this was behind her and she could fully enjoy the evening.

Would that ever happen? she wondered. A real date with him when she was free to enjoy it to the fullest? Somehow, she hoped that would be the case. If it was to be it was a long way off, however, and there was no telling if Sam would even be around by then. She hoped that he would, because Sam was the man she should have met somewhere in her past, or somewhere in her future. And she was truly beginning to regret that she'd met him at this point in her life.

It was a crisp evening, not too cool but a little on the breezy side, and the light reflecting off the pier over the softly rippling waves looked like shards of a broken glass. Della stared into the water for a few moments, mulling over all the what-ifs with Sam, until Janice Newton waved to her from across the street, shattering all the thoughts she shouldn't have been having in the first place. "You look like you might be having a special evening out," Janice said, as she took a seat on the wooden bench next to Della.

"Dinner with Dr Montgomery," she said, trying not to sound as self-conscious as she felt, especially now that certain realizations about her feelings for him were beginning to creep in. Her clothing had finally arrived, and none of it was appropriate. Her dresses were too pretentious for a seafood restaurant, her slacks too casual. She'd settled on a basic black dress, one without much style, and dressed it up a bit with a shawl, which would fend off the slight chill in the air. Then she'd dabbed on a touch of make-up and twisted her hair in a knot at the back of her head, trying for sleek and accepting casual-nice when a few wispy tendrils popped loose. Was she presentable enough? She'd wondered about it as she'd taken one last look at herself. Then wondered why it mattered and why she was being so silly over it. After all, this wasn't a date.

"As in a date?" Janice asked.

"As in an evening out with a colleague. Trust me, my dating instinct is dead. Haven't done it in for ever, and I'm not sure I want to do it again."

"I'd heard you were recently widowed. I'm so sorry, Della. It's got to be tough picking up the pieces and starting over again. Especially here, without friends and family to support you. So, are you officially still in mourning?" she asked, looking at the totally black outfit Della was wearing.

"I mourned for about a day, then got over it. These widow's rags are simply all I have that would be fitting for dinner."

Janice gave her a knowing nod. "Well, as a survivor of a bad marriage myself, I'm not going to ask any questions. I expect we've got some similar war stories to swap but that'll keep for some long, lazy afternoon over strawberry daiquiris and tea cakes. But, Della, in the meantime, if you need someone… I'm here. I know you're really busy up there right now, but any time, day or night…"

"I appreciate that," Della said. "I've been so frantic trying to keep things together I really haven't had much time to make friends. But daiquiris and tea cakes sound wonderful."

"I think practically everyone here considers you a friend. And that's not only because we want you to stay with us.

Which we hope you will. But it's because you're so good with…with everybody, including Stuart Jennings." She laughed. "No one's good with Stuart, but he's come to town singing your praises a couple of times now. I think he's in love with you, and if you can tame that kind of a beast… Like I said, you're so good with everybody."

"Stuart's not so bad. Maybe a little grumpy, but he lives over on his side of the island all alone, and he doesn't even have the benefit of having patients wander in and out to break that loneliness and monotony, like I do."

"His choice," Janice said.

"Maybe, but sometimes when we make those choices we don't look at the long-term outcome of them. If we did, the last two doctors here wouldn't have come and gone so quickly." She paused for a moment, thinking about Anthony as he'd been when she'd married him, and as he'd become over the years. There wasn't much difference, not in him anyway. But in her… "When I was married, if I'd looked very far past the wedding day I probably wouldn't have gone through with it. But we don't know those things at the time, do we? No crystal balls for future-gazing, unfortunately." Except if she'd had that crystal ball to see what her future with Anthony would have turned out to be, she wouldn't have had Meghan. Even thinking about that brought the tears to her eyes.

Janice noticed Della's tears welling, and patted her on the hand. "Life takes some crazy turns, doesn't it?"

"Crazy," Della agreed, her thoughts returning to Sam. "Definitely crazy."

Sam paced up and down the pier, alternately looking out over the water then punching the glow button on his watch and checking the time. He wasn't quite sure when Della would arrive. Wasn't even quite sure that she *would* arrive, even though she'd promised. He'd spent the afternoon with his supervisor, trying to convince him that he needed extra time on Della's report. *She's making steady progress* was what he'd said. Which was a bit of a hedge on his part, because steady could be defined by mere inches or vast miles. But she was making progress, slow that it was, and now that he'd sent for his old medical office equipment her progress was going to surpass mere inches by a long shot. He had no use for all that stuff any more, and there was no reason to keep it in storage. Especially when Della needed it.

Giving it to her was much more involvement than he'd intended, and in the end, if questioned by his superiors about his motives, he would argue that he'd told her his purpose there was to help her get established. The truth was, he really wanted to do that. For whatever reason she was hiding, Della needed her practice to have a good start. Failure would be devastating for her, and he saw that every time he looked at her. So what was the big deal about donating a few pieces of unused equipment anyway? She had a good use for it, he didn't. In his own thoughts he'd already justified it as some of that so-called help he was supposed to offer. In his heart, though, he feared the motive was something altogether different, but he wasn't ready to explore that.

Anyway, he'd made that damned preliminary verbal report that Della's clinic was moving along, wheedled an extra few days to wrap up his dealings on Redcliffe before he reported back to the board, then he'd spent the rest of the afternoon arguing with his ex-wife over signing the papers to release the equipment back to him, since technically she did own half of it according to the divorce agreement. Of course, she hadn't been interested in any of it until he wanted it, then her claws had come out, even three thousand miles away.

Ramona had argued in her truest form for a little while,

then had finally released claim to it when he'd told her that since she demanded half of it, half the past storage bill would be hers to pay. He'd even threatened to leave it all in storage and bill her for half of all future storage fees.

Everybody had their bottom line apparently, and Ramona had hit hers when the threat of paying him *anything* had sunk in. She'd relinquished title, then hung up. "Yes, you're still the same old girl who goes right for the bottom line, aren't you, Ramona?" he said as he spotted the lights from a craft moving slowly into Connaught harbor.

Sam drew in an overstrung breath. It wasn't a date, and if that's what it turned into, it would be a big mistake. "So why am I doing this?" he asked as the boat drew closer. "Why am I doing something I know I shouldn't?"

Stupid question! He was doing it for the same reason he'd arranged to have a whole office of practically brand-new medical equipment sent to Della. And for the same reason he'd gone after an extension on his report. Even though she obviously had so much going on in her personal life, judging from her tears after finishing that phone call, and had no room for him, he was still drawn to her in a way he'd never been drawn to anybody else.

So he'd left the island for a few days to busy himself with other tasks of his job, hoping that when he returned he'd be thinking clearly again. But the whole time he'd been away, he'd missed her. Missed her terribly. "So I'm stupid," he conceded, his eyes still focused on the craft. Stupid, and absolutely captivated even though he'd sworn, with the stroke of the pen that had ended his marriage, he'd never get that involved again.

That involved... He was. And the hell of it was, Della didn't even know it. "Stupid," he muttered, huffing out a nettled sigh into the fresh night air as the ferry chugged its way into dock.

Except for the night when the ladies had brought all the food, and the day after with the leftovers, Della had been eating out of boxes and cans practically since the moment she'd received the phone call about Anthony. This was a nice treat, she decided as she looked at all the smart options on the menu. Amazing how only four months ago she'd eaten like this regularly, and now it was almost as good as Christmas. She glanced across the table at Sam, who had closed his menu and was now staring at her. "I'm not shy," she said.

He cocked an inquisitive brow at her.

"About eating. I'm not shy. Some women might select a tiny dab of something from the menu, but you're paying, and I'm hungry." That was a bit bold, but the smile she was eliciting from him told her it didn't matter. The comfort level with Sam was unlike anything she'd ever felt. She couldn't ever remember being this comfortable with Anthony.

"Ramona, my wife, selected the tiny dabs, then ate half. And her dabs were the most expensive on the menu." He chuckled. "Funny thing was, she was always trying to achieve your size. It was her compulsion. If there was a weight-loss treatment, surgery or diet out there, she was on it. Never worked, though. She always bought her clothes a size smaller, but never quite got all of herself stuffed into them attractively."

"Personally, I like my clothes on the baggy side. A size larger is fine with me. Of course, Anthony didn't like that. He told me I looked like a frump." She smiled as she pulled a slice of fresh sourdough bread from the basket the server had placed on the table. "Which I did. But I worked in a public-health clinic and what I wore to work simply didn't matter. So why bother with the look when comfort was much better?" Dipping the bread in the sun-dried-tomato-infused olive oil the server had poured into a saucer, she ate a rather sizeable chunk—one not meant to impress anybody about a genteel appetite.

"Would you have divorced, do you think?" he asked. "If he hadn't died, do you suppose you would have divorced him?"

If not for Meghan, yes, she would have. But she believed in the tradition of a family, most likely because she'd been robbed of hers so early on. So she would have stayed with Anthony to keep the family together. For a time, anyway. Maybe that seemed a little self-sacrificing, but when Meghan had been sufficiently old enough to understand the subtleties of a divorce, and realize she wasn't the cause of it, which happened with so many young children, she would have left. "Eventually, I might have left him. I rarely thought past the day, though, so I don't know. We'd gotten to the point that one day was as tolerable as the next, not good, not horrible. So I don't know what I would have done."

"You deserve more than tolerable, Della."

"Maybe I do, but I had enough outside involvements that my relationship with him wasn't all-consuming, much to his unhappiness." She shrugged, then sighed. "Like I said, I don't know what would have happened if he hadn't been killed."

"How did he die?" Sam asked gently. "You don't have to tell me if you don't want," he added quickly.

"No, that's fine. It's not a secret. He was in a traffic accident on his way home from his mistress. He simply fell asleep at the steering-wheel. Kind of an anti-climactic end to a climactic life." She looked directly into his eyes. "I didn't even know he was having an affair…or multiple affairs, as I later discovered. I suppose if I'd known, I'd have told him to spend the night there and not drive home when he was so exhausted."

"I'd heard rumors that Ramona was stepping out on me—

with her tennis instructor, with her golf instructor, with her masseur. Didn't bother to check, though, because I didn't care. I was on the verge of a whole lifestyle upheaval anyway, and I figured that, at the very least, she'd have some sort of a companionship once I was gone. But in her defense, I wasn't the husband she'd thought I would be."

"Which was?"

"Rich." He grinned. "I stayed afloat in my medical practice quite nicely, but I wasn't very enthusiastic about it. You know, you learn a little too late what you don't want. Unfortunately, with that bit of revelation *doesn't* always come a second revelation telling you what you do want."

"And you still don't know, do you?"

He shook his head as he hailed the server back to the table. "But I figure if I keep moving from situation to situation, I might find it." He shrugged indifferently, but the expression on his face was anything but indifferent. "Or not. There's something to be said about life in a series of short takes."

"You'll know it when you see it," she said.

"Maybe that's what I'm afraid of, that I will. Maybe I like the short takes."

Della ordered salmon with dill sauce, two vegetables, salad, a baked potato and cheesecake for her meal and ate every last bit of it, along with several bites of Sam's huge mound of lump crab. It was a delicious meal and a splendid way to pass the first true time off she'd had since she couldn't remember when. She and Sam talked more about the pitfalls of bad marriages, about medicine and medical school, about some of the things she hoped to accomplish in Redcliffe. As Redcliffe crept into the conversation, she was surprised to find that she'd actually built some expectations there that had nothing at all to do with getting Meghan back. They were things she wanted to accomplish—breast cancer awareness classes for the women, a small rehab facility for minor physical therapies, wellness classes for the children. She hadn't expected all that to pop out, really. But Sam made it so easy for her to talk about hopes and dreams. She only wished he had some for himself.

Once she'd almost given in to her vow of silence over Meghan, but a second thought about it pulled that part of the conversation off the table and she switched to how marvelously creamy the cheesecake was. She was still too raw to tell him everything, too protective of that part of her life and, most of all, simply too afraid that saying the worst aloud could make it come true. Had she and Sam been working on a relationship other than what they had, she might have been more open with him. The dinner had certainly been conducive enough for that sort of a revelation, but this wasn't that kind of a relationship. So she went on and on about her cheesecake, and after she took a bite of his raspberry torte went on and on about that, too, until Sam hailed the server, paid the bill, and pulled her along to the street.

"Do you want to take a stroll?" Sam asked. "Cecil's given us another hour before he comes to fetch us, so we can either go to the dock and wait, or take a short walk."

Della was simply too full to walk very far, and all she really wanted to do was the worst thing possible after a huge meal—relax, maybe take a nap. She didn't do much of that, and now she was feeling almost drugged with contentment. Contentment—another of the effects Sam had on her. "I'd rather walk over to the hospital and have a look at Bart, if that's OK with you," she said. "When I talked to his doctor this morning, it still wasn't looking very good. Bart was spiking a fever, and there was a possibility they were going to have to open him up yet again to clean out the wound." She shivered involuntarily. The other two boys, Aaron and Marty, were recovering nicely at home now. Aaron was practically back into his old activities while Marty was laid up with casts and splints on his various fractures. He would heal in time, and be as good as new. Bart, however, was still not gaining solid ground, according to all reports.

"It's hard for you to put it aside even for the evening," Sam commented, as they strolled up the main street to the small regional hospital. He held out his arm to her, and she took it. It was almost like they'd been together for ever, it happened so naturally. More than that, it felt so right.

"My career might be a bit in flux right now, but I've always had a passion about it. My parents put away the money for my medical training early on, because even when I was barely toddling I was intent on becoming a doctor. So they decided they'd best be prepared for it."

"Were they doctors?"

"No, teachers. And after they died, it never occurred to me that I wouldn't go through with our plan. I was going to medical school, that's all there was to it. I really didn't have a home in the proper sense after that, but there was always that one goal, and working toward it never let me down. Somehow, that goal still kept me close to my parents, too." Did Meghan think about her now that she was gone, or had that void already been filled by an overbearing grandmother and a new puppy? "Of course, I strayed off the path a bit in my last year of medical school and got married, but even that didn't stop me. I had to become a doctor."

"For me, it was always on my list of top two or three choices. I liked the idea well enough and, because my other choices were so impractical, I suppose I leaned toward medicine because it was the practical thing to do."

"That's right. You wanted to become a novelist, didn't you?"

"Didn't ever make it with that, but I did write some articles for a medical journal once."

"And?"

"They were published. And so boring they even put me to sleep." He chuckled. "So by now you've come to realize that I'm pretty well aimless. But I get by. No complaints, except from the ex-wife who found her true love in a Shakespearean actor who will make ten times the money I ever will."

"Shakespearean?"

Sam nodded. "And very good at it."

Della laughed. "To be, or not to be? The question is, will you know what to aim for when you finally do see it?"

Sam stopped in the middle of the sidewalk, then looked at her in a curious way. "Yes," he said. "I think I will."

According to the nurse on duty, Bart was having a difficult night. His fever was up again, and his breathing was shallow. She had a call out for his doctor, in fact, as Della and Sam strolled up to the nurses' station to enquire. "Mind if we take a look at him?" Della asked, quite well aware that she was not his attending physician.

"Go right ahead, Doctor," the nurse consented rather quickly.

When Della and Sam arrived at Bart's room, there were already two nurses at the bedside, both busy with various duties. One was changing the IV bag and increasing the volume of the fluid going in. The other was taking Bart's vital signs—temperature, pulse, blood pressure. As she pulled the thermometer from his mouth, she shook her head.

"What?" Della asked quietly.

"One hundred four point eight," she said. "Up half a degree in the past half-hour."

"Is he responsive?"

Both nurses shook their heads. "Hasn't been all day," the one hanging the IV bag added. "He's opened his eyes a couple of times, but doesn't follow anything directional, like my finger."

"He's septic," Sam said gravely. Septicemia was a critical condition where the body was literally filled with infection. New drugs made it curable, where only a few years ago it had been a near death sentence. But sometimes even now the drugs simply failed.

"The doctor's on his way in, but it might be another hour," the nurse continued. "He's on a call down in Overby and not able to get away just yet."

A pitfall of a small hospital, Della thought. They shared physicians with other small hospitals. On the upside, care in the smaller hospitals was almost always better and more attentive. She knew Bart was getting the very best care he could possibly get anywhere. Instinctively, she pulled a straight chair over to the bedside and sat down next to the boy. "Bart, it's Doc Della." She took his hand and squeezed it, but there was no response. She hadn't expected one, but she'd still hoped.

"Can you hear me, Bart?" she asked, even though she doubted that he could. "I saw Aaron earlier today. He's doing well. Angry that I won't let him loose to do anything other than go to school, but he'll get over it."

She watched intently for a response, but still nothing happened. He didn't blink, and according to his cardiac monitor his heart rate didn't increase a beat. Nothing. "Anyway, I thought I'd stop by and see you before I go back to Redcliffe. Aaron said he'll be here as soon as you're allowed visitors." This was so bleak it totally deflated the pleasant mood she'd been in only moments ago. She didn't even know the boy, but she felt a connection to him. More than that, she felt him slipping away. Her stomach turned over at the thought and for a moment she feared she might lose her dinner. Swallowing back nausea, Della slid the chair back from the bed and stood. Then she took one final appraisal of the monitors and walked out the door. "It's bad," she said to Sam as they passed the nurses' station. "And I think someone needs to prepare his family." That was the grimmest of realties in the job, especially when it was a child, and although he was sixteen, Bart was still somebody's child…a child she didn't believe was going to make it.

Della left word to have Bart's attending physician call her as soon as he arrived at the hospital then she walked slowly, as if the weight of lead was dragging at her, to the front door. Tonight her thoughts were with Bart. But they were with Meghan, too. She was losing so much of her daughter's life now that she could feel deep, agonizing sympathy for Bart's parents, who were losing so much of his.

Both were tragedies that shouldn't have happened.

CHAPTER EIGHT

DELLA hadn't even laid her hand on the exit door's push bar when the ominous alarm sounded throughout the hollow corridor. "Code Blue, ICU," was the page over the public-address system. "Code Blue, ICU."

It was a horrible, grim call, one every physician dreaded, and a cold chill stabbed her in the spine. Immediately she turned to Sam, and the unspoken truth passed between them. He reached out and squeezed her arm, and then, in that fractured second afterwards, she spun around and ran back to the room from which they'd only just walked away.

Sam stayed with her, shoulder to shoulder, and as they approached Bart's room, where there was already a frenzy of emergency lifesaving activity in its embryo stages, she dropped her shawl and purse on the floor and looked in the window. Even though her heart had felt the sickening lurch of what was taking place in there from the instant she'd heard the call, she still had to see it for herself, had to make sure. When she did, that sick feeling returned to the pit of her stomach, this time nearly doubling her over. Immediately, as if he'd anticipated her reaction, Sam grabbed her from behind to steady her. "No," she whispered, as the red crash cart full of emergency resuscitation supplies was wheeled bedside and the medical equipment already there—pieces not necessary for the next procedures—was shoved back to the wall.

"Dr Riordan!" one of the nurses called. "We need you! We don't have a physician on the floor yet."

No, they didn't need her. The nurses were competent. But Bart needed her, and that's what impelled her in the door and straight into action. "Can you intubate?" she asked Sam, as she snapped on a pair of gloves and handed another pair over to him.

"Haven't for quite a while," he said, then immediately started a search of the crash cart for the proper equipment. He grabbed the laryngoscope and checked to make sure the light on it was working. One of the nurses stepped up to him with an endotracheal tube, and Sam took a quick look. "I want an 8," he said. "He's a big boy and I don't think a 7.5 will do." When she handed him the size 8, he quickly checked the cuff to make sure it didn't leak, then squirted a dab of lidocaine on the tip of it to make insertion easier. "I'm ready whenever you are," he said to Della, who was busy preparing for the cardioversion—the shock to Bart's heart that, with any luck, would restore its normal rhythm. He was in ventricular tachycardia, a precursory rhythm to a much more devastating cardiac episode if they weren't careful.

"I want the tube in before we shock him," she said, then gave the assisting nurse a medication order. "Twenty of procainamide, IV." Another glance at the heart monitor told her that Bart's heart was beating almost out of control now, going on to double its normal rhythm. "Damn," she muttered, and in the span of that single, uttered word his heart rate essentially sputtered out and the trace of it on the monitor looked more like a quiver…the heart was trying to pump but not doing so. Ventricular fibrillation, a herald of death! "Epi," she shouted, countermanding the first medication order. "I want one milligram of epinephrine, push." She glanced over at

Sam, who was connecting the resuscitation bag to the endotracheal tube and giving it a few good squeezes. For someone who hadn't done the procedure in a while, he'd been quick about it, she thought. Quick and very efficient. Briefly, she wondered if he knew what a good doctor he was.

"Epi's in," the nurse said, and Della immediately focused on the tracings on the cardiac monitor again. Nothing! She grabbed up the paddles on the defibrillator and shouted, "Give me 200." The amount of shock, in joules, Bart's heart would receive. When the machine buzzed to indicate it was ready, she shouted, "Stand back!" Then she made sure everyone had obeyed before she shocked his heart. Immediately, she checked the monitor to see if his heart had converted back to a normal rhythm, but it hadn't.

"Push 300 milligrams of amiodarone, then give me 300 joules," Della ordered, then shocked him again. But it didn't work. His heart was still trying to pump, but it simply couldn't. The infection ravaging his body was defeating it, tiring it out. "Give me another milligram of epi, push." With that order, she looked over at Sam, and in the instant where their eyes met, she knew that he knew. This was always the worst moment—the moment of truth. It was the time when so many would call it quits, but for her it was always the beginning of the second push because there were always miracles. She'd seen them happen. "Stay with me, Bart," she said. "Don't give up on me yet." And she wasn't giving up on Bart. "Three sixty joules," she ordered, then prepared for another shock. "And push another 300 of amiodarone. Also, I need a blood gas."

They went round and round for another thirty minutes, alternately pushing drugs and shocking Bart's heart. "Do it again," she yelled after each failed attempt. Then she would hold her breath and watch the heart monitor for any sign of activity. Eventually, even the quivers that showed as erratic waves on the monitor gave out to a very calm, flat sea where nothing moved. No waves, no blips. No sign of life at all.

"It's time," Sam said gently, stepping up behind her.

She shook her head. "No! One more time!"

"Della," he said, bending to whisper in her ear. "It's time." He slipped his arm around her waist to steady her. "We've done everything we can, sweetheart, and I'm sorry. But it's time."

His words took a second to register. When they did, Della drew in a deep breath and stepped back from the bed. She hated this part, and her heart was aching so badly she thought it would explode. She wanted desperately to cry, but she couldn't. Not now. The tears of loss always came later, in a private moment. And she did cry with every loss. But right now she was in charge here, it was her duty to remain strong.

Sucking in another deep breath, Della glanced up at the clock and braced herself for the horrible words. "Time of death, ten-nineteen p.m. I appreciate your efforts here. You're a very good team to work with, and we've done everything we could possibly do. Thank you." Forced words, and so difficult to say. Words that meant Bart Talmadge, age sixteen, was now only a memory. Della took a look at his face—not a boy, not a man. She was hurting for all the things he should have done, and could have done. And she hurt for his family and friends. "I'm sorry, Bart," she whispered to him as the nurses were busy tidying up the room, tossing out the trash, turning off the machines, removing the tubes from Bart's lifeless body. "I'm so sorry."

She watched until the nurse extracted the endotracheal tube from Bart's mouth and pulled the sheet up over him before she turned and exited the room. Pausing outside in the hall, she leaned against the wall briefly, fighting to regain her equilibrium.

"Are you OK?" Sam asked, pulling her into his arms.

"Yeah," she said, even though she didn't sound it. "I really thought we'd get him back." She leaned her head against his chest. "Even though when I'd just looked in on him and thought I knew the outcome…I really didn't know. Or didn't want to believe it."

"Which is why you're a good doctor. You don't give up."

"Neither did you, Sam. I saw the way you worked in there. You're a good doctor. We're a good team."

"It's been a long time," he said, then sighed. "A very long time."

Della stayed in Sam's arms for another minute before she finally pushed himself away. "I suppose I'd better wrap it up," she said. The rest of the procedure was routine. Record the notes in the chart, sign the proper documents. But before that, she had to hear Meghan's voice.

Grabbing her purse, which had been retrieved from the floor, Della fished out the phone card and ran to the nearest public phone. She knew the response she'd get when she called, but she didn't care. The only cure for the ache deep inside her was to hear Meghan's voice. "Hello, I need to—"

"Do you know what time it is?" Vivian snapped. "We were all in bed."

"I need to speak to Meghan," she said calmly.

"Not at this time of the night, you don't. And I have a good mind to report this to the judge."

"I need to speak to Meghan," she said again, still holding onto her outward calm even though inside she wasn't in the least tranquil.

"Aren't you listening to me? I said no! I'm not allowing you to disturb your daughter at this time of night."

"And I said I need to speak to Meghan." Her voice broke this time, gave away a little quiver she didn't want Vivian to hear.

If she did, she would perceive that as a weakness and construe it as yet one more reason why Della was not a fit parent.

"Have you been drinking?" Vivian shrieked. "Is that what's possessing you to be so rude?"

"No, I'm not drinking. I've had a very bad night."

"Which has nothing to do with Meghan. Wanting to wake her up only because you feel like it is irresponsible, Della. But I should expect that from you, shouldn't I?"

Della mustered her strength for the final round, practically biting her tongue to keep herself from saying something she would regret. "Please, allow me to speak to Meghan. I've lost a child tonight and I need to hear her voice. As a mother, surely you can understand that."

Apparently that caused Vivian to relent a bit, because the huff of anger that came across the phone line as a flatulent sigh was accompanied by an ungracious capitulation. "Oh, very well. But just for a minute," she snapped. "And I'm warning you, if you ever do this again, I'll be the first one at the judge's door."

Della shut her eyes, waiting for the next voice.

"Mommy?" Meghan said.

She sounded so sleepy that Della truly regretted waking up her daughter, but she desperately needed the balm of her voice, even if only for a minute. "Yes, sweetie, it's Mommy. I'm sorry that Grandma had to wake you up, but I wanted to hear your voice. I miss you so much, Meghan." She was fighting off all the tears now—the tears of her heartbreak over losing Bart and the tears of her heartbreak over losing her daughter. "I had a very bad day at work, and I thought maybe you could tell me about Scooter. That would make me feel much better."

"He chewed up Grandma's slippers. Both of them."

Score one for Scooter, Della thought. Too bad he couldn't

find whatever it was that caused Vivian Riordan's attitude and have a chew at that, too. "Did you apologize to your grandmother?" Della asked.

"Am I supposed to?"

"Yes, sweetie, you're supposed to because Scooter is your dog. He's your responsibility. If he does something bad, you have to apologize for it since he can't." Tough words, since Vivian didn't deserve an apology for anything. But raising Meghan the proper way had nothing to do with what Vivian did, or did not, deserve. "And when you apologize, ask her if there's something you can do to repay her. That's part of being responsible."

"I will, Mommy. Promise."

"I know you will, sweetie."

"When can Scooter and I come live with you?"

"Soon, sweetie. I'm working on it every day." Every day, in every way. With no guarantees. But she wasn't going to allow that sadness to envelop her while she was talking to Meghan. Nothing and no one would pull her from that moment.

Meghan went on to tell Della about another dog they saw in the park every day, and how she hated eating broccoli and peas and her grandmother's oatmeal, and how she was drawing her mother another picture of Scooter—one with her grandma's slippers in his mouth. Then all too soon it was time for her to go. Vivian was giving Meghan a ten-second warning in the background

"I love you, Meghan. You know that, don't you? There's never a day that I'm not thinking about you all the time."

"I love you, too, Mommy. So does Scooter."

Della listened until the phone clicked in her ear, then she hung up slowly, swiping at the tears on her face—tears of anger, mixed with tears of sadness, mixed with the worst tears of all…tears of loss. Tonight there was so much loss all around her.

As she stood there, willing herself to move away from the phone and return to the nurses' station to deal with the aftermath of Bart's death, Sam's strong arms slipped around her again and pulled her back into him. "I'll bet you're a very good mother," he said, his voice so quiet it blended into the dimness of the empty corridor.

"Not any more," she said, not even trying to mask her pain.

"What happened?"

This wasn't the way she'd wanted to tell him, admitting to being a dismal failure as a mother mere minutes after being a dismal failure as a doctor. But why not? Why the bloody hell not? He already thought her daft for buying her home and clinic. This was another notch on that dubious belt. "They took my daughter away from me after Anthony died," she said, her voice totally flat. "I lost everything, including the house. Couldn't afford a babysitter when I was at work, so I took Meghan to work with me. Lots of mothers do that to spend more time with their child, and I thought it would be a brilliant idea. But it was a public-health clinic and the judge said that wasn't a fit place to keep a child sometimes twelve hours a day.

"And there were times at night I had to drag her out with me on an emergency call. So he granted custody to my in-laws, who'd been working on that almost from the moment Anthony died. They were sneaky about it, like Anthony was always sneaky about his affairs, and I simply didn't see what they were doing. They won, I lost. They were much better suited to raise her, according to the judge. So they were awarded custody."

She turned around in his arms and glared up defiantly at him. "And I really don't care how you judge me over this. You won't think, or say, anything I haven't already, knowing that I wasn't judged good enough to keep my daughter."

"Is it your fault?" he asked simply and honestly.

"No, it's not my fault. I took good care of her even when she was at the clinic. It wasn't the most conventional of lifestyles, but we were managing. And we were starting over, trying to find a new way for ourselves. But the only thing the judge could see was the lack of material things I could give my daughter after she was used to a more privileged life. It didn't matter to her, but it sure mattered to him. I was a good mother. A damned good mother." She let out a deep breath. "I'm sorry," she said, winding down. "I shouldn't have taken it out on you. It's not your concern."

"You won't allow it to become anybody's concern, will you? You're intent on braving it on your own, no help, no friends to lean on, no sympathetic ear."

"It's hard to trust anyone," she admitted. "You do, and they let you down. You depend on them and they stab you in the back. Keeping it to myself means the only one who will let me down is me." It felt so good in his arms, pressed to him, the length of his entire body supporting the entire length of hers. She needed it, which was exactly why she couldn't have it. There was no room for that kind of need in her life. Other than the need to get Meghan back, there was nothing else.

Della pulled away from Sam and stepped back from the phone. "I've got six months to find myself a better situation and prove that I can take care of my child. I thought this would be it, Sam. I bought it sight unseen because the people on Redcliffe subsidized half the cost. I couldn't afford a start-up any other way, and I've never completed a residency, so I'm not exactly a valuable asset out there in the medical market without a specialty."

"Why didn't you tell me all this?" he asked, taking a step forward and pulling her back into his arms.

She went willingly, too willing, laid her head to his chest again and allowed him to support her again. "Tell you what?" she said, suddenly feeling weary to her bones. "That I've been judged an unfit mother and had my daughter taken away? That wouldn't exactly instill confidence in my patients on Redcliffe, would it? I was afraid if anybody found out, no one would come to me. Without patients I don't have a medical practice, and without that I don't have my daughter."

"But they trapped you, Della," he said. "They took advantage of a difficult situation."

"Not really. The people here didn't know my circumstances when the made the offer. I was desperate, but I could have had a look at what I was buying. I did have twenty-four hours in which to decide, and that was enough time to go to Redcliffe, but Meghan was in a play at her kindergarten, and I couldn't miss it. She was so proud to be Sleeping Beauty so how could I not be there to see it? Meaning I took the offer and hoped for the best. So it wasn't the people here. Not at all. They made a generous offer at a time when no one else was being generous to me."

Sam shook his head and drew in a labored breath. "I'm so sorry," he whispered. "I can't even begin to understand how difficult this must be for you."

"I'm sorry, too," she said sadly. "For myself, for Meghan, and most of all right now I'm sorry for the Talmadge family. I can't begin to imagine how difficult this is going to be for them."

"Would you like for me to come with you when you go to tell them?" he asked.

More than anything, she did want that. And she wanted Sam to go home with her afterward. Tonight wasn't a night she wanted to be alone. "Yes," she whispered. "I would like that."

It was such a beautiful day to wake up in such a dismally gray mood. Even having Sam there with her, holding onto her all night, hadn't improved her disposition. Although in those fitful moments when she had managed to doze off, having his body pressed to hers and his arms around her had made her feel better. Even in her bleakest moments, Anthony had never done that. He'd stayed on his side of the king-sized bed, feigning sleep, or protesting that he had an early morning start. As many nights as not when she'd been restless, he'd traipsed off to the guest room. Or, as she'd since learned, to the arms of his mistress.

But last night, with Sam pressed so close to her on a cot barely made for one, for the first time in ever so long she'd felt safe, and cared for. And comforted. At her age, it shouldn't have been such a strange feeling, but she couldn't remember having had it since her parents' death.

"I suppose we should get up before someone comes to the door and catches us," she said, still enjoying the feel of his body against hers. Coffee in bed, reading the paper together, making love…that would have been such a wonderful way to start a gray day together. Or any day, for that matter. But anything more than sleeping in the bed could lead to all of that fantasy, especially the part that had them stretched out naked together, and she didn't allow such fantasies. Although she could almost smell the coffee.

"Already caught," Stuart yelled from the kitchen.

"When did he get here?" Sam whispered.

"Heard that," Stuart responded. "I got here twenty minutes ago, at my appointment time. Decided to fix myself some coffee since you two weren't in any hurry to get up."

"You have odd patients, Doc Della," Sam whispered in her ear. Then he kissed her behind that same ear.

It was quick, and for a moment Della wasn't sure if it was a kiss or merely Sam turning over and bumping into her. But then he raised his hand to brush away her hair and he kissed

her again. It was definitely a kiss! No mistaking that. A kiss
that came with a tingle all the way down to her toes.

Then he simply rolled off the cot without a word and
padded out to the kitchen. "What do you take in your coffee?"
he called back to her at the doorway.

Not exactly the first words she wanted to hear after a kiss.
But what was there to say? He'd given her a wonderfully
romantic little peck and had done with it. That's all there was.

"You sleep with her but you don't know what she takes in
her coffee?" Stuart grumbled. "She takes sugar. Too damn
much sugar to be healthy, if you ask me."

Della laughed. "And you'd better not be taking sugar in
yours, Stuart." A nice cup of coffee and an entire day in which
to shake off her glum mood would have been good, but that
wasn't going to happen. She had appointments this morning,
then she had to check in on the Landers boys later to see how
they were doing now that word about Bart had, no doubt, spread
throughout the entire island. She also wanted to stop by the
Talmadge home to see if there was anything she could do for
them. Last night they'd been steady over the news about their
son, but now, with a new day, and an even newer reality settling
in, it wouldn't be so easy for them. Shock would be giving way
to grief, and they might require some medical support. She
would if she were suffering the raw kind of loss they were.

So, with so much to do on her list for the day, Della rolled
off the cot, took a good stretch, then headed for the bathroom
to splash her face with cold water. On her way, she looked at
the walls, at the floors…all stripped down. That's the way she
felt this morning, and sharing a nice cup of coffee with Sam
and Stuart wasn't going to change that.

"She's in a bad way?" Stuart asked, as he poured a cup of
coffee for Sam.

"It's tough losing a patient, especially a child," Sam replied, rummaging through the cupboard for a loaf of bread and, hopefully, some jam to go on the toast he was going to make. "It's the part of the job you never get used to. You have to do it, but it takes its toll."

"I heard she fought hard to save him. Heard you both did. Also heard you're here to shut her down," he said, straightening up to look Sam directly in the eye. "She doesn't know that, does she? That you're going to do it?"

"Where did you hear so many things?" Sam asked, giving Stuart a tight smile. "On such a small island?"

"I may keep to myself most of the time, Doc, but Stuart Jennings is an international trade mark that gets me out and about every so often. And it's amazing what I hear when I do go. A friend of mine on the health commission mentioned they had someone here on the island who was doing the report on the condition of Doc Della's clinic. She said there's a leaning toward not certifying it to stay open because the man sent here to observe was being rather slow about his observations, and to them that indicates a possibility of problems."

Sam lowered his eyes. "Perhaps he's being rather slow about the report because he wants to give Della an opportunity to succeed."

"Which she is," Stuart retorted. He was a spindly man with deep wrinkles in his face and sparse white hair that stuck out in every direction. He had piercing blue eyes, though. Sharp eyes that didn't miss a thing, and he was narrowing them in suspicion. "She's doing a good job here, and it's nice not to have to get into that damn boat and go across to Connaught for every sneeze and sniffle. We want her to stay here," he snarled. "I want her here, and none of us are going to take too kindly to you getting rid of her, if that's what happens. We might fight you on it, Doc."

"It sounds like we both want the same thing," Sam said, his voice cold. He turned and popped two slices of bread into the toaster. "I don't have a complaint with her work. But I do with patients staying in her kitchen for observation or having a physical exam in her living room. And you know what, Stuart, you get part of the blame for her breaking the law. You, and every other person on this island. You wanted her, and you put out an attractive offer hoping to snare a doctor, hoping the doctor didn't have enough time to properly assess the situation. Which was exactly what happened. Della didn't have enough time."

"But she got a good deal. Sure, the property's not much to look at but she'll bring it up to where it needs to be in time. For now, we're patient. We don't mind the inconvenience so long as we have a good doctor. And she's all that, and more."

"She's an excellent doctor. And, yes, she got a very good deal, but she's working without the means to bring this place up to standard. In case you haven't figured it out, that's what could, and probably will, get her shut down. By law, she cannot practice medicine under these conditions. The board of health won't allow it and there's nothing I can do about that except stall, which I've already done and probably won't be allowed to do again without having another health inspector sent out in my place to have a look. And the next one isn't going to be as lenient as I've been.

"I reported that she's making progress, but by the strictest definition it's not enough progress to keep her open. So if she's shut down, you're without your doctor and Della is without…" Her daughter. "Her job. And the next time she'll be able to reapply to practice will be in six months. Again, that's the law. Not my choice." It would be past her deadline to regain custody of her daughter, too, and being forced out of practice for six months certainly wouldn't help her case professionally or financially. "And I hope you're not going to tell her what I'm supposed to do because I don't want to put more pressure on her than she already has."

Stuart shook his head. "Well, somebody's got to tell her eventually, Doc. But I'm sure not going to be the one to do it."

Sam drew in a deep breath. The whole situation was sticky, and here he was, stuck right in the middle of it, on one hand wanting to help her and on the other duty-bound to write a report that would close her down. "I'd be better-off writing a novel," he muttered, as he pulled the toast out of the toaster and dropped in another two slices for Della.

"What?" Stuart asked.

"Nothing. Just the musings of a brooding mind." And there were more things to brood about than he wanted to admit. So very many more.

CHAPTER NINE

THE morning passed relatively quickly, and when everybody had gone, and after she'd returned from her two house calls, Della wandered down to the cottage with a bucket and a mop in hand, intending to get started on the clean-up, since she did have office equipment on the way. She didn't have another patient scheduled for the next three hours, and there were several things she intended to accomplish in that nice chunk of unplotted time.

Of course, the first chore was cleaning the cottage. It was a formidable task. Her own house was clean now, and she could live with the remainder of the peeling wallpaper, the plastic windows and scuffed floors for quite a while. But the cottage that would be her clinic was different. It had to be perfect, ceiling to floor, and every little nook and cranny in between had to be spotless. John Hesper had taken a look and pronounced the structure fit for its purpose. He'd even tweaked her design for interior renovations and promised to help when he had time, in exchange for medical favors in the future. She liked that—it wasn't charity. They were going to trade their services.

Della sighed wistfully as she stepped into the cottage, set down her bucket and mop, and aimed her digital camera for several *before* shots, in case the judge was interested. "At least it's small, so there's not much to clean," she said, walking over to the window to have a look outside. Sometimes it simply didn't sink in that the wonderful view belonged to her. Did she own any of the ocean? she wondered. Perhaps only an inch or two? Meghan would love that—her own private beach, her own private ocean. Anthony would have thought it silly, of course. That glorious ocean view without a five-star hotel from which to see it wouldn't have been worth his while. "I wasted so much time," she whispered.

"In that case, I hope you're really not going to waste an afternoon cleaning," Sam said, stepping up behind her.

"Depends on your definition of wasting an afternoon, I suppose," she said.

"Anything that starts with a bucket and ends with a mop is a wasted afternoon." Grinning, he nudged the bucket back to the wall, behind the front door. "Out of sight, out of mind," he said, then shoved her mop back there with it.

"But starting with a bucket and ending with a mop gets me that much closer to turning this place into a real clinic, which isn't a waste of time." Turning it into a real clinic unlike what her predecessors had done with it. At first she'd been angry over their neglect. Like her, they'd come here with expectations. But unlike her, they'd left before they'd even tried. Now, instead of being angry, she was glad they'd gone. If they hadn't, this wouldn't be her opportunity, her redemption. Her perfect cure. "I'll bet if I look hard enough I might be able to find you a spare bucket and mop."

He paused for a moment before he answered, the twinkle in his eye almost blinding. She could see it…that look he got when he was plotting. It reminded her of Meghan in a way…that bit of innocence mixed with enthusiasm. Meghan's always involved a way to finagle another cookie or an extra bedtime story. And Della could never resist. *There's something clever going on in there,* she thought, watching him form his own plan and almost looking forward to seeing what it was.

"So here's the deal," he finally said, grinning. "You find me a spare bucket and mop and I'll be glad to use it. But first you've got to find me a spare hour for a walk on the beach. The two of us...together," he added quickly. "In other words, we play before we work. After last night, you need to get away for a little while, clear your head, take in some fresh air. Relax."

"No time," she said. "I really need to wash some windows here and scrub the floor. Also, I do have a few appointments later this afternoon. After that I'm supposed to have a run out to another couple of house calls. Ella Thompson up on the north end of the island is having a flare-up of her allergies. She's made her house into a bit of an allergen-free domicile and doesn't want to come out while the pollen count is high. And there's Steve Glover...he's in the middle of writing the second act of his play, and from the sound of it he's experiencing carpal tunnel syndrome...he writes in longhand. I've got some anti-inflammatory samples for him to try, and he's promised me the pick of his autumn squash garden."

"They'll keep for a little while," Sam said, edging his way out the door, gesturing for her to follow. "The days of warm weather are getting shorter, and nice moments for a walk on the beach are numbered. Just look at it out here. It's spectacular, and I think you should indulge yourself in an hour or two off."

"Indulge *you*, don't you mean?" she said, laughing. "And I thought the deal was for one hour, *not* two."

"If I scrub floors for two hours, do I get two hours with you on the beach?"

"One-hour break. That's all the boss allows. But you'll still owe me two for the interruption." Smiling, Della sat her camera on the kitchen counter and followed Sam outside.

With Meghan, she'd never had a regret about giving in. Spending time with her daughter had been better than anything else she could have done with that time. She had the feeling it would be the same with Sam. "You're pushing your luck, asking for one." She gave her head a playful little shake and wrinkled her nose. "If I were you, I wouldn't try for any more or I might have to add a third hour to your bucket duty."

"You drive a hard bargain, Doctor, but I'll take it. One hour from you, not a minute less." He looked at his watch and actually set the alarm on it. "See. I'm a man of my word, and you've already wasted the first minute of *my* time, so let's get going!" He reached out, grabbed her hand, and pulled her along until they were standing on the beach, halfway down to the surf. Then he stopped and kicked off his shoes, and looked at Della. "Well?"

"Well, what?" she asked.

"Your shoes," he said pointing down. "No self-respecting beachcomber would go combing with her shoes on."

"Just how experienced a beachcomber are you?" she asked.

"I lived in California," he said, as if that explained everything.

"On a beach?"

"About fifty miles away."

She swatted playfully at him, laughing. "At least I lived on a canal. Your nearest water was your bathtub."

"And I never once wore my shoes in it."

As Della's shoes slid off, amazingly so did all the pressures of her life. It was like they'd suddenly melted into the sand. Her constantly tense muscles relaxed, and that bit of a headache that was always on the verge of turning into a pounder eased away. Even the simple act of breathing in the pure salt air without the stress of what to do next was exhilarating. Except for her dinner with Sam, it had been so long since she'd taken time for herself that these feelings were all peculiar to her. Now she was glad to have that time away from her responsibilities, and even gladder she was spending these rare moments with him. For this short while she didn't want to be a doctor. She wanted to be plain old Della Riordan, no responsibilities or worries allowed. "I've never really taken a stroll past the first guest cottage," she admitted. "I know I've got quite a bit of property beyond there, but I haven't had time to take a look. Do you think we could wander down that way and see what's there?"

"You're too hard on yourself," Sam said gently, as he took hold of her hand and led her down the beach in that direction.

"And if I'm not, well, you know the consequences. Losing all truly means losing all." She smiled sadly, thinking about the Talmadge family. They truly had lost all last night. She wondered if they'd ever had the time to stroll along the beach together.

"I know I told you last night, but I want to say it again. You were amazing in Intensive Care, Della. You might not have had a chance at a medical specialty, but no one would know that from the way you responded. So, why didn't you go on?"

"Motherhood. I was pregnant during my internship, and barely got through that when Meghan was born. Afterwards, I was otherwise involved with all the baby chores. I did work part time at the clinic, but I spent most of my time with my baby, then, as she got a little older, I added a few extra hours to my work. I always meant to go back and study to become a pediatrician, but it never worked into my plans. Which is fine. I love general practice. A lot of doctors don't want to do that these days—they want to be specialists. But I like being a plain old GP. And since you're repeating compliments, let me repeat mine. You were brilliant with the intubation. I think it's a loss that you don't practice medicine any more. Have you ever considered starting up again?"

"Yes, but not strongly enough to make me do it. I just

didn't have the commitment I needed. And, to be honest, I've enjoyed the little bit I've done here with you far more than anything I ever did in my own practice."

"Maybe you were in the wrong specialty," she said.

"I think it goes deeper than that. To be the best technician at what you do you need to have the passion for it. I never did. My doctoring skills were good, but I lacked the heart to go with them and my patients deserved that as much as they deserved my skills."

"It's hard to imagine you that way," she said. "Anthony didn't have the heart. Actually, he did, but it was a cold heart. He felt no compassion, and apart from the fact that he liked to keep his record as a doctor clean, I don't think he even cared much about his patients. For him it was all about ambition." She laughed. "And there I was, spending my time in a free clinic. I think I embarrassed him."

"Then it was his loss."

"And medicine's loss is not having you, Sam."

"Oh, it still has me. Just not in a way most would consider normal."

It was a beautiful time of the day for a stroll along the water's edge. The sun was bright, but not quite so hot now that summer had ebbed and autumn was nipping at its heels. For the first little while, as she and Sam strolled and talked, Della kept her head down, watching the sand, looking for shells she could gather. Every now and then she bent down to pick up one for her collection, and after she had a pocketful, Della finally turned her attention to the row of cottages dotting the property at the end of the sand. Some were set back further, others were closer to the actual beach. And none were so close together that they intruded on any other.

"I think they're yours," Sam said, running up onto the front porch of one to have a look in the window. "Not bad," he shouted. "It's pretty much the same design as the one you're turning into the clinic. With a little work it could be quite cozy."

"With a little work, like everything else I own," she said, discovering one cottage set back into a thicket of trees that looked to be in much better repair than the rest. Its white paint was fresh, the red petunias hanging in a basket on the porch thriving, and the white wicker rocker still rocking a bit, as if someone had only now darted out of it. Which, as it turned out, was the case.

"Hello," Roger McMurtry called from his front door. "I figured you'd be round sooner or later to collect rent. Saw you two coming up the beach so I thought I'd better get it ready for you."

Della blinked back her surprise. "I have a tenant?" she asked.

"Not only a tenant," Roger said, "but one who pays his rent promptly." He handed over the envelope. "I'm assuming the arrangement will be the same as the one I've had."

Della peeked into the envelope expecting to find a pittance, and nearly gasped at the amount. "Are you sure about this?" she sputtered, as Sam stepped up behind her and slid a protective arm around her waist. She was still so stunned by the five hundred dollars she didn't notice Sam's gesture until after she'd counted the money a second time.

"Actually, it's quite cheap. But the people who used to stay here were all artists, and as a bunch we're not exactly affluent, so none of the owners were too tough on us. Unfortunately, over the years, the us dwindled to only me." He smiled sheepishly. "Repair and upkeep issues. I never cared about having a go at a leaking pipe or a weathered clapboard. But the others who were here felt differently. It was their loss, though. Just look what I'm getting for my rent." He gestured to the wide expanse of the ocean just at the edge of his front yard. "An artist's paradise."

"You say you're good with pipes?" Della said, that proverbial lightbulb of an idea coming on.

"Quite good."

"How would you feel about exchanging some pipe work for the credit of a month's rent?"

"Very good," Roger replied, smiling. "Just tell me when and where."

"I'll do that, Roger," Della said, fanning herself with the envelope full of money. "I'll surely be doing that soon."

"I had no idea," Della said to Sam, after they had walked further on down the beach, out of sight of the cottages. She sat down in the sand and counted her money again, then quickly tucked it away as if it might catch on a breeze and drift off to sea. "Too bad the other cabins aren't in shape to rent out."

"Della Riordan turned landlord?" Sam sat down next to her. "You'd want to do that?"

"Anything to stay viable," she said, leaning back on her elbows to take in the sun. "Besides, leaving all these cabins empty is such a waste. I mean, look at this view. People should be enjoying it."

"You should enjoy it more."

"I will," she vowed. "In good time. So tell me, Sam, how long are you going to be here? You've been here going on to two weeks now, and I thought you'd have other places to go, other doctors to help."

"I do, and I have been doing that, off and on. But I like it here, which is why I keep coming back. Until I'm off this assignment, I think it's a good place to stay."

"Want to rent a cabin with an extraordinary view?" she asked, laughing. "I know a nice little place with a nice little landlord."

He laughed. "If I could I would. But I got to keep a permanent residence more centralized to my district. You're practically on the outer edge."

She had a hard time picturing Sam anyplace but here. Actually, she didn't know him anyplace but here, and this suited him, she thought. He simply looked happy. "But you could come here to write your novel. Roger does his paintings. And somewhere on the other side of the island, Stuart is turning out some of the most noted pottery in the country. I think it's probably a pretty good place for expressing creativity."

"But the minute I move in, you'll get some crazy notion to run off to be an artist like Dr Bonn, then what will I do?"

Laughing, she replied, "Pay me rent until I can sell the place." She was feeling so much better now. Almost feeling light and giddy. She was making a little money, and recruiting people to barter their services to help her. Maybe getting away from time to time to put a different perspective on things was a good idea, because right at this very moment everything about her life didn't seem so bleak. "This could be a very nice place to live, I think."

"You sound as if you're not committed to staying here yet."

She wasn't sure when the actual commitment to stay had happened. Perhaps it had been the very first moment she'd arrived here, when the Brodskys had presented her with their ailing baby and trusted a total stranger to care for her. Or maybe it had been when the women had brought food or when Sharon Farnham had gathered up a stack of home fix-up books for her. Or maybe it had been her last look at Bart Talmadge, and being the one with him at the end. Somewhere along the way she'd come to realize that she wanted to stay here. More than that, she wanted to raise Meghan here, and not as a last resort because it was the only place they could go, but because it was their home…their real home. "Oh, I'm staying. I just meant that it might be a nice place to live if you came here of your own choice. Which I did, totally. But now that I've decided I like it here, I think it might have been fun to simply stumble upon all this, fall madly in love with it, buy it and settle down, instead of having practically no other option than buying it from a description from a solicitor."

"There would be a difference?"

"Maybe. I think stumbling across the next phase of your life has a wonderfully romantic quality to it. But no matter. I'm not leaving here when I get Meghan back. And until that time there's no place to go except back to Miami. But it's so difficult living close to her and not being her mother." And even more difficult living so close to the Riordans, which would be the case if she didn't get Meghan back. Returning to Miami and forever watching from afar the bit and pieces of her daughter's life. Always there but never a part of it.

Sam turned toward her, and brushed a bit of sand from her cheek. "You'll always be her mother, Della. That's not ever going to change, no matter how close or far apart you two are. And Meghan knows that. So does her grandmother."

His brief touch sent shivers of desire running through her. But more than that, his words pulled her to him in a way she'd never been drawn to another man. She wanted to kiss him, be kissed by him… She longed to get caught up in the romantic fantasy she'd almost woven for herself.

Della shut her eyes briefly, willing herself to fight off the mood, but there was nothing in her that wanted to resist Sam, or resist the feelings she was having for him. Nothing at all, as she leaned over to him, snaking her hand behind his neck. She looked into his eyes…beautiful eyes, eyes with such depth she could lose herself in them for an eternity… Then she smiled as she dropped her face down to his.

It was a hard, swift kiss—so full of need she shocked herself by it. But she needed it, needed him, even if only for this moment on the beach. Where the kiss began and where it ended, she couldn't remember later, but she did remember the aching intensity of her lips as they sought his. And the taste of his—so sweet she was greedy for more of it, like a child was greedy for a candy.

Della succumbed to the quiet mastery of his lips as he returned her kiss, and his tongue sent a new flood of shivers and desire racing through her…a flood that threatened to break through her levee of control. Shocked now by her response to what she didn't want, and what she wanted so badly she thought she'd die without, she welcomed his first kiss, and demanded his second, her tongue meeting his and teasing the delicate tip until the sensation caused her toes to curl down into the sand and her nipples to strain against the thin cotton of her white T-shirt.

Sam's hand slid under the T-shirt to discover her peaks, and his eyes opened in surprise when the palm of his hand met her bare flesh. A guttural groan escaped him as he kneaded her breasts, and a wispy groan escaped her as she arched back to enjoy his journey.

He explored for a moment, then removed his hand. All too soon. Della opened her eyes to find him inching up her shirt so delicately it felt more like the nip of a gentle breeze. Once the shirt had barely cleared her breasts, he bent to take one nipple into his mouth.

"Oh," she gasped, starting to feel another kind of tingling elsewhere. Biting her bottom lip to stifle what she was afraid would be much louder, she leaned her head back and stared at the blue sky as Sam licked, then sucked, then nipped gently with his teeth. Such a simple thing to do, and one that nearly had her crawling out of her skin for wanting more.

But he stopped, then laid her back into the sand, and took his place over her. Raw instincts took over and Della wrapped both her arms around his neck then twined her right leg over his left, and fitted herself into the perfect position under him. "Your ribs?' she asked in a husky voice.

"Fine. Just fine."

The feel of Sam pressed to the full length of her was fine, just fine, too. The sensation of his erection crushing into that sensitive area between her legs, definitely fine again. Funny, but she couldn't remember this kind of need. Not ever. But even before they'd shed clothes, and as she was starting to find her rhythm with him, the screech of a seagull overhead split the mood like a sharp knife severing it. Immediately, Sam rolled off her and over onto his back in the sand. "Well, that was getting pretty intense, wasn't it?" he gasped, drawing in a ragged breath.

Della pulled down her T-shirt to cover her bare breasts, fighting for control over her own breathing. Intense? Another five minutes and it would have been an afterglow. Quite simply, she didn't know what to say to him now, didn't know how to respond to him, or to what had almost happened. So she didn't. Sprawled out in the sand next to Sam, she shut her eyes, trying to will away the feelings of utter frustration that were lingering, and the little twinges of pure lust that weren't yet letting go of her.

She'd been so close to allowing more than she could give. Damn it! She'd been on the brink of committing an almost unpardonable act, and save for the squawk of a seagull she would have allowed it, even demanded it. And she'd started it! What had that been about anyway? "I'm sorry," she finally sputtered. "I didn't mean for that to happen."

"It seemed like you meant an awful lot of it." Sam rolled over on his side, dug his elbow into the sand and propped his head on his hand. Then he grinned at her. "Bet it's been a long time since you let your emotions and needs rule your head."

She couldn't look at him. Not yet. "And you can see why I don't. Just look where I end up when I do."

He chuckled. "I like where you end up." Then he reached over to stroke Della's cheek, but she brushed his hand off and sat up.

"I have a little girl, Sam. The only relationship I want is the one I have with her. And until I can have that back…"

He sat up, too. "And what about your own needs, Della? You have them, you can't deny it. I was there, remember? I felt some of those needs in a pretty acute way just now."

She shrugged. "They don't count. Just hormones."

"But they do," he whispered, then he stood and offered her a hand up. "And you're not the type of woman who allows her hormones to take control."

"You don't know what kind of woman I am," she replied. Della stared at his hand for a second, thought about refusing him, then took it. Immediately, that jolt of electricity went shooting through her, even more now than it had before. It would have been so easy to pull him back down into the sand and finish what she'd started, but he was wrong. Until her life was straightened out, none of those needs counted. "I might be exactly the kind who allows her hormones to overrule practicality."

"Or perhaps the kind who forces practicality to overrule her true heart? I think that's the way it is with you, Della."

Della gave him an odd look as she brushed off the sand. "My true heart is only for my daughter," she said.

"Maybe that's what you think right now, but I think there's more to your true heart than you know," he replied.

Della and Sam gathered a few more seashells on the return walk, and she took painstaking care to keep the conversation between them off anything personal. They speculated on the kinds of little creatures that might have once used those shells, talked about what it could be like to invite assorted artists to the beach cottages when, and if, they were ever put back into repair, and they even chatted about the various boats and ships they could see offshore, mulling over where they might be going. But there was no talk of *them*, not about their interlude on the beach, not about what was in their hearts, not about anything they might have together. For Della, such talk only added to the heartache, because she was beginning to think she might be falling in love with Sam. And she couldn't have it. Not at all.

CHAPTER TEN

FIVE grueling days from the first day she'd taken the bucket and mop to the clinic, Della was finally beginning to see the progress. Real progress. Her walls were framed in now, thanks to John Hesper. Not complete, but framed, and to her they looked to be the skeleton of what would be awfully good. Roger McMurtry had updated the plumbing, and she'd bartered the exterior paint job with Quentin Lund. He'd taken one of her front-yard statues—one with fish—to place in front of his seafood restaurant because he thought it would be quite an eye-catcher for island tourists.

So it was all coming together nicely, especially now that the office equipment had arrived. Sam's office equipment. She'd found an old invoice wedged in the back of a drawer— this was all his, every last piece of it. Somehow that made her office feel all the more special. And it didn't even matter that it was going into a tiny space—a postage stamp sized waiting room with a consultation office not quite that large, two exam rooms barely large enough for one table, one patient and one doctor, and finally two very small overnight observation rooms. There was going to be a lot of use crammed into a small area, but cozy wasn't bad because in a very sentimental way— one she shouldn't be allowing but couldn't help—she would be cozy with Sam.

Sam had been around intermittently, and he'd made good on his promise to wield bucket and mop. His presence hadn't been substantial, though. More like in and out. No more temptations on the beach like before because they were never alone. People were coming from everywhere to help now, spending their precious spare time to help. She missed Sam when he wasn't there, though, and missed time alone with him when he was. Missed him like crazy. But his absence, as well as their drifting apart, were for the best. She was so close to a finish in her clinic, she couldn't afford the distraction.

"OK, I think it'll be fine in the corner," she said to Roger and Matt, who were maneuvering her desk into the yet-to-be-walled-off area that would eventually become her office. Right now it was designated by ceiling-to-floor studs all nailed securely into place, as were the rest of the designated areas. "Right over there, in the corner." Which was the only place the desk would go, since any other spot would impede the opening and closing of the office door.

"How soon until you get walls?" Matt asked, lowering his end of the sturdy mahogany desk to the floor.

"A week or two, depending on John's schedule." She smiled. "And after the electrical wiring is upgraded." Which Sheila Jackson was going to do next week in exchange for vaccinations for her children and one night of babysitting so she and her husband could have a date on the mainland. "In the meantime, I'm going to hang sheets between the rooms for privacy." That wouldn't offer much, but it was as good as they'd managed in the clinic in Miami—one thin cotton curtain between beds.

As the desk was set into place, Della snapped a picture, then another when the file cabinet was maneuvered into the other corner, still amazed that all this was hers. It was the first time in her life that she could claim ownership of anything, and thinking about it caused a lump to form in her throat. This was going to be a real life after all. Not a make-do for the next five years, but the real thing. Della Riordan was alive and well on an isolated little island in an isolated little medical clinic.

"Well, you'd better hope *he* doesn't have a problem with sheets," Stuart muttered from the far end of the room. He was in the process of doing a finger stick to test his blood sugar. "Or he'll make your life a living hell over it."

In just the short time Della had been on Redcliffe, Stuart's blood-sugar readings had regulated. Granted, he'd spent more than his fair share of nights on a cot in her kitchen so she could watch him, but his medical progress was steady, and she was pleased. "Do you mean Sam?"

"Who else? He's the only one here who gives a damn about such things, the bastard."

"Is your blood sugar high?" she asked, concerned about his grumpiness. He was normally a little grouchy, though good-naturedly so, but this seemed much too real and extreme, even for Stuart. He was truly out of sorts, which worried her.

"None of your business," he snorted, then hid the glucose meter in his pocket as Della went over to have a look.

"Give it to me, Stuart," she said, noting now that his color was a little ashen.

"A little over two hundred," he snapped.

Della blinked. The low one twenties was normal. Two hundred was getting awfully high. "How much over?"

"Not much. I'll just go take a shot of insulin so you don't have to be bothered with me."

She held out her hand for the meter. "Give it to me, Stuart."

He looked sheepish. "Mind your own damn business."

"You are my business," she said. "And if you don't give it to me, I'll take it." She was getting *really* worried now.

"Fine," he snapped. "Suit yourself, but it's your own funeral if you take care of me, I tell you."

One look at the reading and Della fought back a gasp. Six hundred! Stuart didn't tolerate high readings, and this was extreme. She could bring it down with insulin, but his blood-sugar reading was so high she was going to have to do it gradually. Or else risk a stroke. "No shot," she said. "IV this time, Stuart. Back to my kitchen."

"Over a few lousy candy bars," he muttered.

"How many?"

"Five, maybe six. Not all at one time."

Frustrated, Della shook her head. "I ought to send you over to Connaught Hospital for this."

"Yes, you ought to. Or he'll shut you down for keeping me in your kitchen again. Like I told you, it's your funeral if you do."

"Are you still talking about Sam?" she asked, clearly puzzled by this. Maybe Stuart was a little more out of his head than she'd thought. Elevated blood sugar could do that. Still, Stuart wasn't fond of too many people, so maybe this was merely some animosity about Sam that she hadn't known about. Animosity brought to the surface by his medical condition.

Right now, though, animosity or not, he needed immediate treatment, and Connaught was too far away and too risky for the trip over there. "Could a couple of you men carry Stuart over to my kitchen?" she asked, glad Sam wasn't there to see it. Right now, she didn't need another argument. Not with Stuart in such a dire condition.

"The bastard," Stuart snarled again, as two of the men crossed their hands over into a chair and carried him out the door.

He'd calm down once his blood sugar level was better, Della decided thirty minutes later as she taped up his IV and covered him with an extra blanket. He was already asleep, which was for the best. He needed his rest.

So did she, even though it was barely evening yet. But the days were much shorter now, and darkness came early. Having Stuart there meant she couldn't go out and leave him, which meant she could either work in the house or settle in for the evening. Work was definitely the better option, but this time she chose rest and settled into a chair near the fire, propped her feet up on a stool and simply shut her eyes.

In the distance she heard the sound of Sam's SUV. It was familiar now, a sound she looked forward to, but hadn't heard so often lately.

Suddenly, it occurred to her that she looked a mess. Normally that didn't matter, but she hadn't seen Sam at all for a couple of days, and she wondered if she had time to take a quick shower. Impulsively, she dashed into her bathroom and turned on the water. By the time it had heated sufficiently, she could hear him in the living room, but that didn't matter. He could wait. After all, she'd been waiting for him for days now.

"The bastard returns," Stuart grunted.

Sam looked at the IV hook-up and cringed. It had to be reported. The bad along with the good. He'd been dreading tonight for days but he couldn't put it off. Not any longer. The edict was in and he had no time left.

"I see you're in your normal good mood," Sam replied.

"I'd be better if I didn't know what I know about you."

"Trust me, I'd be better if I didn't know what I know about me, either."

"But you're going to do it, aren't you, Doc? You're going to close her down."

"That's not my decision. It never has been. I only make the report."

"And what's the report going to say?" Stuart asked.

"That she keeps patients hooked to IVs in her kitchen."

"Which will get her shut down."

"Probably," Sam said, shaking his head. He'd been in Boston, trying to persuade his superiors to give him another week. One more week and she'd have a perfect clinic. But the answer had been an emphatic *no*, with the addendum that if he didn't do it, they'd send somebody else who would. Sam knew that only one look would close her down for sure, because none of the hard work she'd put in would be visible. The next inspector would see Stuart in the kitchen, his IV hooked overhead to a pot and pan rack, and that's all he would see.

"So lie about it," Stuart said, his eyes getting heavy again.

As tempting as that sounded, he wouldn't. And right now he despised this job. It was necessary. He understood that. But he'd never expected it to become such a heavy burden.

Turning, he started out of the kitchen and saw Della standing on the other side of the doorway, her hair wet and curling into little ringlets. "Is it true?" she asked. "That you're the inspector I've been dreading?"

He nodded.

"And you've been lying to me all this time?"

"Not lying, Della. Doing my job."

"Which is to shut me down."

"Which is to report on the conditions of your practice. That's all I do. Report what I see."

"A man with an IV in my kitchen. Is that on your report, Sam?"

"I can't lie about it."

"But you know how hard I've been working. You've been here. You've helped me. That's your medical equipment in my clinic. I found an invoice tucked away in a drawer. That's a lot more than merely reporting, Sam."

"Because I didn't want you to fail, Della. But I've warned you that your medical practice couldn't be operated this way.

And I've helped more than I'm allowed to, probably to the point my job is in jeopardy. You didn't listen, though." He gestured to Stuart. "Instead of sending him to the hospital, you've kept him here again."

"That's why he was trying to hide his condition from me, isn't it? He knew what you were doing. And he knew that if he stayed here again, you'd report it." She shook her head and droplets of water sprayed across Sam's chest. "He told me you were going to shut me down if I took care of him. So by saving Stuart's life tonight, I fail."

"But you know you can't operate a medical practice under these conditions, Della. I've been trying to tell you that for weeks. If you'd fixed this place up first—"

"I've already seen dozens of patients, Sam, so what was I supposed to do? Turn them away? Tell them my kitchen wasn't good enough, so please come back later?" She sucked in a sharp breath. "One of the conditions of me being here is that I treat people. If I refuse, I lose the practice. And I'm smart enough to know who needs to go over to Connaught. I send them, Sam. When they need it, I send them. You know that!"

Sam ran his hand through his hair in bitter frustration. "I know it's not your fault, Della. You got caught up in a bad spot. But I've already had an extension, and now my report is overdue."

"Damn it, Sam, this isn't fair. I'm so close."

"You can appeal a decision. Or reapply for status in six months."

"And lose Meghan in the meantime. Which is what's going to happen once the judge knows my right to open a medical practice here has been revoked by the state board."

"I can talk to the judge, explain the situation to him."

"And say what? That Meghan's irresponsible mother spent every last dime she had buying a medical practice she was banned from operating because the facilities were in a deplorable condition and she didn't have the good sense to take a look at them before she signed the contract? Do you really think that will win him over…convince him I'm a fit mother for my child when I'm not even a fit doctor for my medical practice?"

Sam took several steps toward Della and she took several steps back. "Look, Della, this isn't the way I wanted it to turn out. You should know me well enough by now to believe that. I came here not caring one way or another, but now I do care."

"Which does me no good. Why didn't you warn me, Sam? If you really cared, why didn't you say something? The least you could have done was to tell me what you were doing—that you'd put me on some kind of deadline. But you misrepresented yourself to me. How could you do that?"

"I didn't misrepresent myself. You've known all along I worked for the state board of health. I told you that the very first day."

"You said you were assigned to see if I needed help. I thought you were here as my advocate, not my judge."

"I did help, Della. I've helped with patients, helped with your clinic, given you my equipment…"

"Then after all that you've gone back to your room at Mrs Hawkins's and written in your report that I wasn't capable of taking care of those things for myself."

"No, I didn't do that." He didn't blame her for being angry, but he'd held out a thread of hope that their relationship would stand for a little something right now. Which, apparently, it did not. And that stung. He deserved some of this, but not all, and of all the people he knew, he'd honestly believed Della would realize that once she was over the initial shock.

Perhaps he'd been right every time he'd told himself he shouldn't be getting involved. Right now, it seemed like a very big mistake. "I wouldn't do something like that, Della, and you believing I could... I thought we were better friends than that," he said. Much more than friends.

"So did I, Sam," she snapped, then headed down the hall to one of the bedrooms.

"Another lovers' spat?" Stuart mumbled.

"Not even close," Sam replied, then slammed out the front door.

She was too numb to feel anything. Too numb to think. Too numb to draw a normal breath. The committee had been meeting behind closed doors for the past hour, and she'd been sitting on a straight, uncomfortable wooden bench on a cold marble floor, waiting. Sam was in there, of course. He was giving his report, telling them all the things that were wrong with her medical practice. She'd had two days in which to cool down, two days in which to think it through. Two days without walls in her clinic, and two days with Stuart Jennings in her kitchen.

Yes, it was Sam's job to do this. While she didn't have to like it, when cool logic had taken over, she'd realized that. She'd even understood why he hadn't been able to tell her he'd been the inspector. Standards of practice were important and so many things could be hidden if the inspector were to be announced. But all the reasons aside, this still felt like one more betrayal, and all the logic in the world couldn't ease that pain. She'd actually fancied herself falling in love with him. Maybe that's what hurt the most. She'd gone and fallen in love with yet another man who was bound, even if through duty, to betray her. She didn't hate him for it, but the pain of it was almost as bad as the pain of losing her daughter.

In the end, maybe it was she who'd betrayed herself by thinking that she could work it out—medical practice, getting Meghan back, having Sam in her life. Perhaps that was the biggest betrayal of all, thinking that she could actually have it all. And now, sitting in the uncordial, lifeless corridor, waiting for yet another verdict to be pronounced over her life by yet another person who didn't know her, she wondered if she even had it in her to try at another start.

"Della?" A voice came from the other end of the hall.

It was Sam. He was simply standing there. She thought he was waiting for an invitation to approach her, but she didn't look to find out. Instead, she twisted on the bench so her back was to him.

His hollow footsteps clicked slowly down the hall, going from soft to loud, the closer he got. Funny how even now her heart skipped a beat when he was near. It had been doing that for a while, and she'd been trying to ignore it. Today, she couldn't. In the long list of her betrayals, her heart was now at the top.

"They want to see you," he said, stopping several meters short of her.

"Is there any reason?" she asked, still not turning.

"I made my report. Beyond that I don't know."

Finally, she faced him. "In that report, do you make recommendations?"

He nodded.

She didn't ask what they were because she couldn't bear to hear them from him. "You know, all I ever wanted to do was practice medicine and get my daughter back. Somewhere along the line, though, I actually thought I had a right to some hopes and dreams. Looks like I was wrong again."

She stood, and as she brushed past Sam he grabbed her by the arm. "It's not personal," he said.

"Well, forgive me if I take it personally, Sam. Because for me, it is personal." In so many more ways that it should have been. She wrenched free of his grip and marched into the hearing room.

Like the corridor, it was cold in both temperature and ambience. Gray walls, gray chairs, a single table at the front with three chairs, and in those three chairs two men and one woman, all dressed in appropriately muted business suits. Della shivered as she walked forward.

"Please, have a seat," the older of the two men said, then pointed to the single chair sitting across from the table. It was alone in the aisle, making the intent abundantly clear. This was a stark, passionless meeting, not a friendly chat among medical colleagues. "You, too, Dr Montgomery. Please, have a seat."

Della twisted enough to see Sam standing in the back of the room, leaning against the door, his arms folded across his chest.

"I'll stand," he said, without so much as a blink.

He was as starchy as she wanted to be, but her knees felt like jelly, and as much as she wanted to stand, too, she couldn't for fear that at some point she'd wobble on down to the floor. So she sat, and felt horribly uncomfortable with Sam's scrutiny from the rear and *their* scrutiny from the front.

"First, let me say that we appreciate you coming here today." The name on the badge of the man speaking was Dr Mays. He was elderly and distinguished-looking and she wondered if he'd ever practiced medicine or only sat as an administrator of it. "We've had Dr Montgomery's report and gone over it, and now we'd like to ask you some questions."

Like if she still had a patient in her kitchen, she was guessing. Della nodded her understanding but didn't speak.

"So, let's get started," Dr Mays continued. "And I'll be the one to lead off."

Della nodded again.

"According to Dr Montgomery's report, you do not have a functional clinic or office set-up yet. Is that correct?"

One more nod. She was beginning to feel like a bobble-headed doll. "I'm in the process of setting them up, Doctor. But as of today, no, I do not have a functional clinic or office."

"And yet you're already engaged in the practice of medicine?" Dr Quillen asked. She was very staunch-looking. Perhaps the staunchest of the three.

"I was engaged in the practice of medicine within minutes of my arrival. I had a patient in need that I could not turn away."

"Even without the means to give that patient your best care," Quillen stated.

"No, that's not true. My best care comes from my efforts on behalf of my patients, and has nothing to do with my surroundings. The means to give my patients the best care is my experience, Doctor."

"But you're aware that treating patients on a continual basis in a substandard structure is against all guidelines and laws." That was a statement, not a question, from Quillen again.

"Yes, I am aware of that. Which is why I've been working diligently to increase the standards of the building in which I intend to have my clinic." Straightforward questions so far, and while the attitude of the board was rather terse as a whole, she didn't feel any particular bias for or against her. Suddenly, she wanted to turn around and look at Sam. Wanted his support. Needed it. It was something she'd so depended on and not having it now felt like a gaping hole in her heart. "I have digital photos that document the progress, if you'd like to see them." She pulled the CD from her briefcase, stood, and carried it over to Dr Mays, who took it, gave her a gracious nod, then popped the disk into his laptop computer.

The marvels of modern technology, she thought as he clicked into the first set.

The other two doctors scooted in closer and watched as he breezed through photo after photo. She watched their faces for a reaction, but nothing happened until they were about a minute into the display, then Dr Mays exited the photo program, returned her CD and shut the lid of his laptop.

"There are more photos than you have seen," she said, a sick feeling now beginning to creep into her stomach. They'd already made their decision and this was merely a formality, something to lend the appearance of fairness. Della grabbed hold of the table for support. "You couldn't have seen the progress on the clinic. It's further in."

"No need, Dr Riordan. Dr Montgomery supplied us with sufficient photos."

She hadn't seen him take them. Not once. This time she did look at Sam, and he was watching her so intensely she could almost feel the sting of his scrutiny bore right through her. "Dr Montgomery was very good at his job," she said, turning back to face the panel. "All this time I never had an inkling of what he was doing. He deserves to be commended for his efficiency."

"He was," Dr Bruce, the third of the trio, said. "This morning, as he handed in his resignation."

"His what?"

"My resignation," Sam said from the rear of the room. "I turned in my unbiased report, and along with it my resignation."

Della blinked her surprise as Sam walked forward. "Don't do me any favors," she whispered, as he stepped up to stand behind her. "You've already nailed my coffin, so your little gesture isn't going to do you any good."

"His little gesture defended hospitalizing patients in your kitchen, Dr Riordan," Dr Quillen said. "And treating them in the back seat of your car. His little gesture brought with it letters from grateful patients." She picked up a small stack of papers. "The mayor, a family named Landers, a family named Talmadge. Stuart Jennings called us bastards to even think about shutting you down, and as long as I've know Stuart, that says a lot. He doesn't like people generally."

Della blinked in surprise yet again. "They need a doctor on that island. In the short time I've been there, I've seen one hundred and seventeen patients, twenty-nine of whom were house calls. And, yes, I've hospitalized Stuart in my kitchen a few times, but if I hadn't done that he wouldn't have gone to Connaught for treatment, and he has a condition that needs constant treatment."

"You understand that we do have to abide by the laws of the state," Dr Mays said. "We cannot bend them merely because you present a compelling need. Everybody has a compelling need, Doctor. But your patients have a need, too…to be seen in an appropriate setting."

"I understand." She couldn't tell whether this was sounding bad or good, and in nervous anticipation of the coming verdict she bit her lip.

"Your clinic conditions do not meet minimum standards and you cannot be allowed to practice there until they do. In addition, you cannot treat people in your home because, like your clinic, it's not up to standard."

Bad. Definitely bad.

"But we do realize the need for medical services on Redcliffe. We've long realized that," Dr Quillen interjected. "Which is why we've come up with this decision. We're going to waive the six-month waiting period and allow you to reapply when your clinic is set up properly. Naturally, we'll be sending someone other than Dr Montgomery to do the next inspection, since he's no longer in our employ, and if you do not succeed at that point, we can't grant you any more leniency."

Della nodded. This was sounding better.

"And as for your patients," Dr Bruce interjected. "House

calls. That may be a hardship on you for now, but it's not your
medical skills we're faulting. All reports indicate you're an
excellent physician. It's the facility in which you administer
those skills that is lacking, which is where our sole jurisdic-
tion lies, Doctor. We trust that you'll make the most of this
situation."

Dr Quillen leaned forward as an aside. "And as a warning,
if your patients need watching, they have to go to Connaught
until such time that you have the proper facility. And that goes
for Stuart. I talked to him a little while ago and told him if
he's caught in your kitchen for anything other than a meal,
you'll be shut for good. Sam fought like hell for you, Dr
Riordan. Don't let him down."

"I won't," she said, not sure whether to laugh or cry. "I
won't let any of you down."

"We're counting on that," Dr Mays said, then picked up a
file folder and opened it. It was clear that this matter was over.
She was still the doctor of Redcliffe Island.

She really didn't want to go inside. Not yet. It was a sweet
victory, and she wanted to celebrate. She'd thought it would
be with Sam, but he'd hurried out of the hearing room without
saying a word, and by the time she'd made it to the hall he
had been nowhere to be found. Of course, she deserved that.
All those bad things she'd said, and thought… Sam had put
his job on the line for her. Quit it so he could step out of his
objective shoes and fight *like hell* for her.

But he wasn't here now, and after she'd stepped off Captain
Cecil's boat she'd gone straight to Mrs Hawkins's to see if
he'd come back there. He hadn't. Mrs Hawkins had said that
Sam had checked out.

So that was that. She'd got what she wanted, and lost so
much more than she'd ever known she'd wanted.

The cool night breeze stirred around her and Della shivered. Sam was right. The days of warm weather were getting shorter, and nice moments for a walk on the beach were numbered. She wanted to walk now, but there was such melancholy wrapping around her that the sheer effort of putting one foot in front of another was almost more than she could endure. For the first time since she'd come to Redcliffe, she felt totally, utterly alone. Something had sucked the life out of everything surrounding her and a dispiriting bleakness was settling over her beach like a heavy gray fog.

Tonight, for the first time, she fully understood how the other doctors had felt here. The isolation was overpowering.

So why hadn't she felt this before now? And why was she feeling it now, on the night she'd achieved such a victory?

Because this was the first night she was truly without Sam. He'd been with her in some way since the very first moment she'd arrived. And now he wasn't.

"You picked a fine time to realize how much you love him," she muttered as she forced herself to trudge out to the shore. The bits and pieces of those feelings had been there, and she'd always known if she put them together what she'd find. But knowing that, and knowing what she did now were vastly different. Sam was not only the man she loved, he was the man she wanted to love. "Except you've done nothing but push him away from the start," she said as she kicked off her shoes.

The sand was cool tonight, and as she walked along, she felt the tiny seashells newly washed ashore under her feet. But she didn't stoop to pick them up for Meghan. Not now. Tonight was only for her, to rejoice over her victory and cry over her loss.

Somewhere down the beach a tiny light glowing in the dark caught her eye. Probably Roger out enjoying the view. It would be a lovely way to spend a perfect evening like this, she thought, watching the stars, listening to the waves lapping the shore. A lovely way she should have spent an evening with Sam.

She really didn't want to go over to Roger…didn't want to interrupt his solitude, and didn't want him to interrupt hers. But she wasn't ready to turn back yet. So she decided to walk on by him at a distance, offer him a friendly greeting, and keep going. As she got near, Della could see his silhouette in the small bonfire he'd built. He seemed larger than she thought Roger to be, more like the way Sam should look, sitting there.

Of course, she was being silly. She wanted to see Sam sitting there. That's all it was. Wishful thinking. Sam was gone now, and she'd gotten her way about it. No involvement whatsoever.

Wistfully, Della kicked through the sand as she circled around behind Roger. Her eyes down, she said her obligatory hello without slowing down, but the returned greeting caught her breath.

"Sam?" she whispered, stopping and turning to look at him. "I thought you'd left the island."

"I'd intended to," he said. "Packed up, even got as far as the dock. If Captain Cecil had been there I'd be in Connaught now, but he was having supper on the mainland, so I had some time to wait. Funny how waiting brings on thinking. Hadn't meant for that to happen, but it did."

"About me?" she asked.

"No," he said, rather matter-of-factly. "I've already done a lot of that. Tonight it was about me."

Della thought about going over to the fire to sit next to him, but he hadn't invited her and she wasn't sure he would even want her there, so she stayed where she was, where she could see only his silhouette against the glow of the embers. "What about you?" she asked.

"The usual things. Where am I going? What am I going to

do? What do I want to do? It happens when you've just resigned your job...all those uncertainties sneaking in."

Uncertainties she knew only too well. "You didn't have to resign," she said.

"Of course I did. In order to testify as your advocate and be subjective about it, I couldn't do that and maintain my position as an inspector. Professional ethics and all."

"Did you like your job, Sam?" she asked.

"No. Not particularly. It's just what I was doing during that part of my life."

"And the next part?"

"That's what all this thinking is about. I know the next part, and I want it to be the permanent one. You know how, in medicine, if we can't make that definitive diagnosis we start going through a whole list of rule-outs? You rule out one thing then another, and hopefully when you've ruled out everything that it isn't, what's left is what it is. I've been ruling out for an awfully long time, Della. An awfully long time."

"So what's left on the list?" she asked. "What's the one thing you haven't ruled out in your diagnosis?"

"You," he said, again matter-of-factly.

"How could you?" she gasped. "I mean we haven't even..."

Sam held out his hand to her. "Maybe we should, with our very own rule-out list."

Della took his hand and dropped down into the sand with him. "Actually, I think I'd rather work on a rule-in list with you. Try it, and if we like it, keep it on the list." She reached out and brushed his cheek. "And there are so many things I want to rule in, Sam. Things I didn't know I could, things I've always been afraid of. I'm damaged goods, Sam."

"And I'm a doctor who knows how to heal the damage." He leaned over and brushed her lips with a soft kiss. "Starting with a night spent here on the beach...our first *real* night together."

The two of them together on the beach. Definitely her perfect cure. "I love you, Sam," she whispered as she settled into his arms. "I know I've been difficult, and I've put you off, and I've said some things—"

He raised his index finger to her lips to shush her. "My night, remember? No apologies, no regrets, Della. I fell in love with you the moment you stepped off the boat and there have been no regrets since then."

It was her night, too, the one she'd wanted more than any other night in her life. No apologies, no regrets. No fears. "I love you, Sam," she whispered as they settled down on the beach blanket together, watching the stars overhead and listening to the gentle lapping of the waves licking the shore. In the distance, the lonely, mournful horn of a freighter making its way to port sounded, but tonight Della wasn't lonely or sad. Not any more.

"Remember the last time we were on the beach and I wasn't wearing a bra?" she asked.

Sam moaned. "I've remembered that many times."

"I'm not wearing a bra tonight, Sam."

"I thought you'd never ask!"

CHAPTER ELEVEN

"I'M GOING to throw up," Della moaned, sinking down onto the bench outside the courtroom. The hall was stark and dismal, almost emblematic of her mood these past few days, knowing that today it was all or nothing.

"Morning sickness again?" Sam asked, rubbing her belly. At four months pregnant she wasn't showing even the slightest tummy bulge yet, but he rubbed her belly dozens of times a day anyway. "Can I get you something?"

"Not morning sickness. Just nerves, and I'm fine. The only thing I need is Meghan." Sam had been an absolute rock these past months, putting up with her moods over Meghan as well as her pregnant hormonal moods, while trying to adjust to his own new life. "Are you happy, Sam?" she asked, suddenly feeling weepy. This little mood swing happened about ten times a day, and he was always so good about that, too. "I mean, look what's happened to you all of a sudden—new home, new job, pregnant wife who's always in a mood swing."

He leaned over and kissed her on the cheek. "And I wouldn't have it any other way."

He was writing now. They'd set up one of the cottages as his retreat, and when he wasn't seeing patients—he practiced medicine with her on a part-time basis—he was down the beach, doing what he'd always wanted most to do. She thought he was writing a medical thriller, but he wouldn't tell her yet. Most likely it was about some wonky lady doctor who lived on an isolated island and went totally bonkers without the man she loved. Without Sam, *she* would have gone totally bonkers.

Della wiped a tear from her cheek, then sniffled. "Neither would I," she said as a new splash of tears started down her cheeks.

"So maybe that's the question I should be asking you. Are you happy, Della?"

She looked at him through her blur of tears and instead of answering she let out a strangled sob then threw her arms around his neck and stayed there for a minute, until Sam nudged her away. "I think you need to calm down before they call us into court," he said, pushing back the hair from her face. "If the judge were to see you now, he'd think you were miserable." Smiling, Sam gave her a gentle kiss. "Of course, I like you with a red nose and blotchy cheeks. Looks good with the blonde hair."

Della pulled a tissue from her purse and blotted her eyes. "I don't know how many children you want, but this is what you're going to get every time," she said.

"So they're tears of happiness?"

She felt those happy tears start to puddle behind her eyes again and drew in a deep breath, trying to stave off the next deluge. "What if it's not enough, Sam? The house is wonderful now, the clinic set up and thriving. But we're not exactly setting the world on fire financially, are we? And that's not going to improve much for a while." It didn't matter to her that it wouldn't. But it could be a pivotal point for the judge. He might look at everything she considered a success as a failure. And the fact that Sam wanted to adopt Meghan might not sit well with him, either. Sam had talked to Meghan as much as she had over the months, and had gone with Della to Miami twice for a visit. The relationship between the two had been instantaneous and amazing. Legally or not, Sam was already her father.

But how would the judge see that? Would he see that as unfair to her late husband? Or to the Riordans?

There were so many questions and uncertainties, and when they dragged her down, Sam was always there to pick her back up. The most amazing thing was that she hadn't realized how absolutely miserable she'd been in her first marriage until she'd realized how absolutely happy she was in her second. And happy was such a good place to be.

"Our lot in life..." He smiled. "Good lot, Della. Very good lot."

That got her to weeping again and Sam pulled her back into his arms. Six months ago, when the judge had taken Meghan away from her, this wasn't anything like she'd expected her life to be. Back then, she hadn't been able to think in terms of good. But now it was all good, except the part where Meghan was missing from it. That's what still scared her. As good as it was, it would never be perfect until somebody was living in that pink and purple bedroom she and Sam had been working hard on for the past couple of weeks. "But I'm afraid the judge isn't going to see how good it is."

"Everything you've done these past months is nothing short of a miracle, Della. He'll see that."

"You're biased."

"I have a right to be." He reached down and rubbed her belly again. "Can't wait until you're fat," he said, grinning. "I have a huge bias in favor of women who are carrying my child."

"You're going to make me cry again," she warned.

"Picking out paint colors makes you cry."

"Dr Riordan," a clerk called from the entrance to the court room.

Gasping, Della took hold of Sam's hand. "Would I look awfully bad letting you carry me inside? Because I'm not sure my legs are going to work."

"You'll do just fine," he said, steadying her on their way to the courtroom door.

"I need better than fine," she said, as they took their seat down near the front, at the hearing table. "I need brilliant, and I'm afraid the judge isn't inclined to think that raising my daughter on an isolated island is going to be…" In the rear, the rumbling of people entering the room stopped Della, and she spun around to see the source of the racket. Mayor Vargas, the Talmadge family, Aaron and Marty, Gina, Janice Newton, the entire Brodsky family, and…Stuart Jennings. All in all, she counted fifty-three people, people who had come from Redcliffe Island in Massachusetts to Miami, Florida, to support her. Naturally, that started the tears flowing. "They all came for me?" she asked, on the verge of a sob.

"Of course they did. Friends don't let people they care about go through things like this alone. And they are your friends, Della."

"Our friends," she corrected, swiping back a tear. "They're *our* friends, Sam." She blew a kiss to the crowd, then turned back as the Riordans entered the room, walking right past her without so much as a cordial nod. That cold fact slammed her reality back into place. The last time she'd been here they had walked away with her daughter. Sucking in her breath, Della gritted her teeth for what was about to come.

"I've been going over the report, Dr Riordan," the judge began after he took his seat a minute later. "Or should I say Dr Montgomery, since it seems you were married a few months ago."

Della nodded. It already sounded ominous. "Yes, Your Honor, was married. And either name is fine." Fine until Meghan had the Montgomery name, then they would all be Montgomerys. For ever. That was the only outcome she could think of.

"And congratulations are also in order since, according to the records, you're going to have another child in five months." He gazed rather curiously over the top of his glasses at Della. Vivian gasped at that bit of news. Della had not told the Riordans yet.

"Thank you," she said to the judge. "In five months, Meghan will have a baby brother or sister."

He nodded stiffly. "Now, about the custody matter…"

Sam reached over and took Della's hand.

"Let me clarify a few facts, if you will. First, you are married to a…" He glanced over his papers then looked up at Della. "An unpublished novelist?"

"His book is under consideration by a publisher. And he does practice medicine, Your Honor. We're partners. I'm the full-time associate, he's part time, and he will take full coverage for me when I'm off for my maternity leave."

"And it says here that you run an artists' colony?"

"We have three artists in residence presently. We're currently renovating cottages to take in several more. Before I bought my property it had been an artists' colony, and we're trying to restore it to its original condition."

"I've also checked your financial records—"

"We're solvent," Della interrupted hastily. "Not wealthy, but we get by."

"For heaven's sake, they live in a shack on a beach," Vivian blurted out. "The woman's unstable. She was married four months after my son's death, and now she's taking in artists in her spare time. My granddaughter deserves better than that."

"It's a renovated Victorian cottage on the beach," Della corrected. "Fully renovated."

The judge glanced toward the back of the courtroom at the Redcliffe residents. "It's not your intention to be represented by legal counsel for these proceedings?" he asked Della.

"My legal counsel did me no good the first time I was here, Your Honor. I lost my child when he represented me, and I didn't see any good sense in paying him to come back and represent me that way again. I believe that the truth will speak for itself."

"It certainly will," Vivian piped up.

The judge gave Vivian a stern look, then said, "We'll proceed."

"Just stay calm," Sam whispered to Della. "It's almost over now. You're going to have Meghan back in a few minutes."

She shut her eyes, said a quick prayer, then looked at Sam, smiled, and mouthed the words "I love you" as she braced herself.

"Dr Della Riordan Montgomery," the judge began. "I started by looking at all the photos you documented. Two thousand of them were an excess, but I did scan the majority and the first thing that struck me was the condition of the property you purchased. Based on that, I wondered if you were capable of making sound decisions. The place was horrible. I read testimony from the agent who arranged the purchase of it, and when I learned that you'd bought that monstrosity sight unseen…let's just say that if you'd had a custody hearing at that point I would have revoked your parental privileges permanently. Children need their parents to make better decisions than that you appeared capable of making."

Across the aisle, Vivian snorted aloud.

"I read testimony from the health commission stating your right to practice in your clinic was almost revoked, then I took a good hard look at your financial situation. These are all factors that could have easily stacked against you, but I saw the progress, and for the past fifteen minutes I've been listen ng to your friends—friends who traveled on their own to attest to how fit you are to regain custody of your daughter. They're staunch admirers, Doctor, and they spoke of the value you've added to the quality of life on the island. That's glowing testimony. Of course, there were many other things to be considered besides that, the most important being where your daughter would be better off living, with grandparents who can provide amply for her or with her mother, who has displayed some rather questionable and some apparently admirable moves."

He glanced at the Riordans. "You've done well with Meghan. I had a chat with her moments ago, and she's a happy, well-adjusted little girl."

Della drew in a stiff breath, and felt Sam's hand tighten on hers. The verdict was about to come down.

"But she's a little girl who wants desperately to live with her mother and the man she calls her new daddy." He looked back at Della. "It's not always about the worth in material assets, Doctor. It's about the worth of a family, and your family has worth. I hereby grant you the return and permanent custody of your daughter. You've created a new life in which she'll thrive, and I wish you the best of luck." With that, he banged the gavel, bringing the hearing to a close.

Stunned, Della didn't breath for what seemed an eternity. Didn't breathe, didn't move, didn't even blink for fear that if she did she would discover this to be a dream. But Vivian's voice shouting her protest of the verdict snapped her out of that and when she did finally blink, she realized she truly had everything she needed to make her life perfect. "Sam," she whispered, as he pulled her into his arms. Then the tears flowed again, and didn't stop even outside in the corridor, when the court clerk brought Meghan around.

Della dropped to her knees and pulled Meghan into her

arms, and cried the tears of the happiest woman in the world, for now she truly had it all. "We can go home now," she choked. "All of us."

"And Scooter can stay in my room?" Meghan squealed, as she jumped up and down on her pink and purple bed.

Della pointed to the dog bed tucked into the corner—a pink and purple one Sam had made. "That's his new home, sweetie. He can stay right there."

"And I don't have to go live someplace else again?" she asked. "Not with Grandma and Grandpa?"

"You'll be going back to visit them, but you're living right here," Sam said, setting Scooter down on the floor. "If you like pink and purple." It was a tough decision for Della, allowing Meghan to return for visits to her grandparents' home after all they'd done, but for Meghan it was the right decision because they were her family.

"I love pink and purple!" she cried.

"Then it looks like you're staying." Sam got down on his hands and knees and crawled over to Meghan, who jumped off the bed and wrestled him to the floor. As they tussled about on the pink and purple shag rug Mrs Shanahan had made in exchange for payment on her account, Meghan squealed in delight, grabbing Sam around the neck and trying for a piggy-back ride. Through it all, with Sam and Meghan and Scooter in a pretzel twist romping about on the floor, Della simply stood back and watched her family. It was amazing how good it felt, being happy. And she was happy. Laying her hand on her belly, she smiled. This was everything she'd ever wanted.

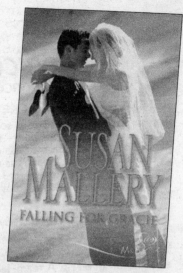

First comes love, then comes marriage...

That was Gracie's plan, anyway, at the ripe old age of fourteen. She loved eighteen-year-old heart throb Riley with a legendary desperation. Even now that she's all grown up, the locals in her sleepy town won't let her forget her youthful crush.

...but it's not as easy as it looks.

And now she's face-to-face with Riley at every turn. The one-time bad boy has come back seeking respectability – but the sparks that fly between them are anything but respectable! Gracie's determined to keep her distance, but when someone sets out to ruin both their reputations, the two discover that first love sometimes is better the second time around.

On sale 1st September 2006

Can you tell from first impressions whether someone could become your closest friend?

Lydia, Jacqueline, Carol and Alix are four very different women, each facing their own problems in life. When they are thrown together by the hands of fate, none of them could ever guess how close they would become or where their friendship would lead them.

A heartfelt, emotional tale of friendship and problems shared from a multi-million copy bestselling author.

On sale 18th August 2006

FREE!

4 Books
and a surprise gift!

We would like to take this opportunity to thank you for reading this Mills & Boon® book by offering you the chance to take FOUR more specially selected titles from the Medical Romance™ series absolutely FREE! We're also making this offer to introduce you to the benefits of the Mills & Boon® Reader Service™—

- ★ **FREE home delivery**
- ★ **FREE gifts and competitions**
- ★ **FREE monthly Newsletter**
- ★ **Exclusive Reader Service offers**
- ★ **Books available before they're in the shops**

Accepting these FREE books and gift places you under no obligation to buy, you may cancel at any time, even after receiving your free shipment. Simply complete your details below and return the entire page to the address below. You don't even need a stamp!

YES! Please send me 4 free Medical Romance books and a surprise gift. I understand that unless you hear from me, I will receive 6 superb new titles every month for just £2.80 each, postage and packing free. I am under no obligation to purchase any books and may cancel my subscription at any time. The free books and gift will be mine to keep in any case.

M6ZEF

Ms/Mrs/Miss/Mr ....Initials ....

BLOCK CAPITALS PLEASE

Surname ....

Address ....

....

....Postcode ....

Send this whole page to:
UK: FREEPOST CN81, Croydon, CR9 3WZ